DETROIT PUBLIC LIBRARY

D0830069

IF IT ISN'T
LOVE

CHANDLER PARK LIBRARY
12800 HARPER
DETROIT, MI 48213

IF IT ISN'T LOVE

DWAYNE S. JOSEPH

Urban Books
1199 Straight Path
West Babylon, NY 11704

If It Isn't Love copyright © 2009 Dwayne S. Joseph

All rights reserved. No part of this book may be reproduced in any
form or by any means without prior consent of the Publisher, ex-
cepting brief quotes used in reviews.

ISBN- 13: 978-1-60162-189-4
ISBN- 10: 1-60162-189-2

First Printing July 2009
Printed in the United States of America

10 9 8 7 6 5 4 3 2 1

Distributed by Kensington Publishing Corp.
Submit Wholesale Orders to:
Kensington Publishing Corp.
C/O Penguin Group (USA) Inc.
Attention: Order Processing
405 Murray Hill Parkway
East Rutherford, NJ 07073-2316
Phone: 1-800-526-0275
Fax: 1-800-227-9604

Acknowledgments

God . . . as always, thank you for life.

My family and friends . . . Love you all!!

To Portia . . . let's do it big in '09!

To all of the readers and the book clubs . . . Thank you for always supporting my efforts! I appreciate it! Here's a story to quell your appetites until "Betrayal" comes out! As always, continue to hit me up with your feedback!

To my DEFENDING SUPER BOWL CHAMPS!!! Big Blue all day . . . EVERY day!! Let's keep it going!!

Much love!

Dwayne S. Joseph

www.myspace.com/Dwaynesjoseph

djoseph21044@yahoo.com

And the Pharisees came to Him, and asked Him, is it lawful for a man to put away his wife? Tempting him.

And He answered and said unto them, What did Moses command you?

And they said, Moses suffered to write a bill of divorcement, and to put her away.

And Jesus answered and said unto them, For the hardness of your heart he wrote you this precept.

But from the beginning of the creation God made them male and female.

For this cause shall a man leave his father and mother, and cleave to his wife:

And they twain shall be one flesh: so then they are no more twain, but one flesh.

What therefore God hath joined together, let no man put asunder.

And in the house His disciples asked Him again of the same matter.

And He saith unto them, Whosoever shall put away his wife, and marry another, committeth adultery against her.

And if a woman shall put away her husband, and be married to another, she committeth adultery.

Mark 10: 2-12

IF IT ISN'T LOVE

PROLOGUE

"You have six months to live. Up to a year . . . possibly, with medication, but we caught it late, so the more realistic time frame is six months. I'm sorry."

Jean Stapleton-Blige sat stoic in Dr. Johnson's uncomfortable chair on the other side of his desk and stared. Not at him. Not at anything really. She just stared.

Leukemia.

Chronic Lymphocytic Leukemia to be exact. CLL for short.

Six months to live.

Sure, extending her life beyond that was possible, but there'd been no confidence in the doctor's tone.

Jean stared at nothing. Dr. Johnson cleared his throat. He'd given news like this many times before, but the delivery was never easy. Life was unfair. Damn unfair.

He cleared his throat. "There is chemotherapy or other drugs that you can try."

Jean averted her gaze from nothing in particular, to Dr. Johnson's somber, brown eyes. "That won't cure me, will it?"

"No."

"And the likelihood of living past six months is slim, correct?"

Dr. Johnson nodded. "Yes."

Jean stood up and gathered her coat in her arms. "Then there is no point in trying anything. Thank you, doctor. I'm glad to have met you."

Jean extended her hand. Dr. Johnson looked at her and tried to conceal his frown. Sixty-five years old; still a lot of life left to live. Damn unfair, he thought again. He stood up and took Jean's hand. He wanted to apologize again, but instead said, "Good-bye, Mrs. Stapleton-Blige."

Jean nodded and then turned and walked out of his office.

Minutes later, she sat in her car in the parking lot, again staring at nothingness. Tears should have been flowing from her eyes. Her hands should have been shaking. She should have been cursing God for allowing this to happen to her. But none of those things happened.

Jean breathed slow breaths.

Death was inevitable, and at some point it happened to everyone. Some people's time came before others. Whether she liked it or not, she'd caught the early bus. There was no point in being angry or sad. It was what it was. For better or worse, Jean had lived her life, and now God was telling her that her time was up and He needed her at His side.

She let out a slow sigh. Six months. Somehow she

knew that she'd never make the year time period. She leaned her head back and stared out of her window and looked up toward the clear autumn sky. Her home, she thought, looking past the clouds. In six months.

She sighed again and thought about her husband, Stewart, and wondered how he would handle the news. As minister of the largest Baptist church in the city, Stewart often gave sermons about death and how it had been something not to grieve over, but to celebrate because it meant going to sit beside the Lord to do work for Him. Jean couldn't help but wonder if he would see it that way when she broke the news to him.

Her life with Stewart was envied by many women. Handsome with lazy Marvin Gaye-like eyes, a chiseled jawline, and deep baritone voice, from the time they'd begun dating to now, women longed for his attention. Unfortunately, he longed for theirs as well, and over the years, that longing never wavered. So while Jean played the good wife and smiled on the outside, she cried daily on the inside, because despite Stewart's infidelity, Jean loved her husband with all her heart and that love kept her locked in a marriage in which she'd never really been respected. She'd always been just "The First Lady of First United Baptist." That was her moniker.

Stewart was the sole breadwinner in their home. His mission of spreading the Lord's words put them in the six-bedroom house they lived in. His sermons paid the bills, put the expensive clothing in her closet, and allowed her to drive the Mercedes she was sitting in. Stewart had never come out and voiced it, but his actions clearly showed that as far as he was concerned, as long as he provided for his wife and children, he had every right to engage in his extra-marital trysts. After all . . . his romps with other women had meant nothing. It was just sex. All Jean had to do was keep the house clean, raise the children, and do all of the things that a minister's wife was supposed to do. And that's just what Jean did. 'Til death do us part; that was the vow she'd made years ago, and unhappy or not, she would abide by that promise.

Jean sighed again.

What would he say when she told him? Would he change his ways? Did it even matter?

And what of her children? What would they say?

Her daughters, Monica and Karen, with whom she had very strained relationships, and hadn't spoken to in months—what would they say? What would their reactions be? And her son, Jeffery—how would he deal with the news? Jean couldn't remember the last time she'd spoken to her youngest. How would he react to the news? Would he still want nothing to do with her, which had been the last words he'd said to her?

Six months.

Jean looked at the clouds and watched them amble by within the clear blue. Against her will, tears slowly escaped from the corners of her light brown eyes. She wiped them away, but the flow remained steady. A passerby would mistake them for tears of sadness, but they were hardly that at all. Sadness could not bring the flood.

But regret could, and did.

Jean Stapleton-Blige started her car while tears ran down her cheeks. Six months. That was the time God had given her to close the wounds of regret for things

4

done and undone, and words said and unsaid. Staring up at the clouds she realized that.

As she cried, Jean smiled. She was going to die, but before that eternal sleep came, she would repair her relationship with her family. That determination brought her a comfort and peace she hadn't felt in a long time.

Leukemia.

She couldn't help but wonder . . . had this been God's punishment or gift?

1

Monica was running late. Again. She was always doing that. She couldn't show up anywhere on time. School, weddings, dates, work; Monica was late even by CP (colored people) standards. But she wasn't taking the blame this time. It was Karen's fault that she'd slept through her alarm clock and its incessant whining, and woke up with a splitting head-ache that she prayed the four Advil she'd taken would get rid of. Monica hadn't meant to stay out so late. But after Karen dropped her unexpected bomb, going home early had become out of the question. Older by two years, her sister was pregnant. Monica was going to be an aunt.

Never one to overdo alcohol, when Karen delivered the news at the Cheesecake Factory, Monica and their girls Tatiana and Natalia took more than one celebratory toast of champagne. No longer able to drink with the best of them, Karen had water.

Monica threw clothes around her disheveled bedroom and searched frantically for her car keys. As she did, the festivities from the night before with her sister ran through her mind.

"I'm pregnant, girl," Karen had announced with a smile.

Stunned, Monica said, "Run that by me again."

Rochelle, the loudest of the bunch never gave Karen a chance to repeat. "She said she's pregnant!" she screamed.

"How many months?" Monica asked.

"Two months going on three. I had no clue because I only just missed my period."

"Oh my God!" Monica screamed, hugging her sister. "When did you find out?"

"Today."

"What did Alex say?"

"I didn't tell him yet."

"Why not?"

"I want to wait for the right time. You know he has that baby mama drama going on with Mariah. I have to make sure he'll be okay with this."

"Sheeit," Tatiana interjected. "He better be okay with it. You gon' be a mommy, girl!"

The ladies screamed as Monica hugged her sister again. "You sure you're ready?"

"Ready? I'm twenty-nine. It's about time, don't you think?"

Monica smiled again and gave her sister another hug, then put her hand on Karen's belly. "I'm going to be an auntie!"

The ladies screamed out loud again and lifted their glasses for a toast. They didn't care as the other diners looked at them with annoyed glares, although Tatiana, the most ghetto-fabulous of them all, took a brief moment to say out loud: "Do you people mind if we celebrate without y'all being all up in *our* business?"

It may have been bold and borderline rude, but that was Tatiana, and she got her point across because the staring ceased.

The recollection of the previous night faded when she finally located her keys beneath a small pile of clean clothes sitting on the floor beside her dressing table. She had a meeting at ten o'clock and she had to brief her team on the plans beforehand. She grabbed her makeup bag as she bolted into the bathroom and hurried to apply her makeup. When she was finished and satisfied with her rapid beautification process, she grabbed her black blazer from her unmade bed and slipped into it. Before rushing out of the room, she checked herself out in the mirror. She had to admit: she had it going on. She was attractive even without the makeup. Her C-cup breasts were perky and her ass was tight. To make the package even sweeter, she was educated, independent, strong, and earned one hell of a salary. No wonder Bryce was hooked.

Monica blew a kiss to her reflection and took a quick disappointing glance at her room in the mirror. Clothes everywhere, bed unmade, random things scattered on the floor, dressing and night tables. She had to get her room and the rest of her apartment together when she got home. She hurried out of her room, closed the door behind her, and swore to do that, just as she had for the past two months.

Keys in hand, coat grabbed from the back of her sofa, Monica was about to run out of her apartment when the phone rang. For a moment she thought about letting it go to her answering machine, but then figured it was Bryce calling to wish her good luck, which he usually did before big meetings. She moved to the phone, grabbed the phone from the base, and hit the talk button.

"Hey sexy!"

"Excuse me?"

Monica snapped her head back a bit. "Mama?"

"Is that how you answer the phone?"

"I thought you were Bryce, Mama."

Her mother hmph'd. "Bryce or not, you should still answer with a hello."

Monica rolled her eyes and cursed herself for not looking at the caller ID first. "Mama, I don't mean to rush you but I was just on my way out the door."

"Hold on, girl. Can't you spare a few minutes for your mama? We haven't spoken in three months."

"I really can't, Mama. I have a big meeting today."

"You puttin' work before me, girl?"

Monica sighed. She didn't need this right now. "Mama . . . it's a big meeting. The biggest of my career."

And it was.

As a creative director for one of the biggest advertising agencies in Washington, DC, the meeting she was going to have, was a very big deal. With top draft picks, a new coach, and a new attitude, the owner of the Washington Redskins wanted a new advertising campaign. With a fresh approach, he and his partners wanted every home game to be sold out, and they wanted to double what they sold in merchandising. If Monica and her team delivered the way everyone had been counting on them to, then chances were very good that the Redskins account would be placed in their laps. It was an extremely lucrative opportunity that the CEOs of her company had been solely focused on, and that excited Monica.

At five foot five, and 128 pounds, she loved a challenge. She always had. The bigger the obstacle, the more determined she was to conquer it. She'd gotten that trait from watching her mother succumb to the challenge of her father, a man she spoke to once, maybe twice a year. Without ever meaning to, Monica's mother showed her and Karen what type of shit they weren't going to take from any man. And it didn't matter if he worked for God or not. A dog was a damn dog, and Monica never liked pets. The fact that her mother put up with the dog that called himself her father, and everyone's minister, bothered Monica to no end. She loved her mother, but didn't respect her, because her mother didn't demand it for herself. And that created vast distance.

Monica's father was the reason she and Karen didn't go to church. Why should they go and listen to a minister spread the word and talk about how wrong it was to sin, when sinning had been second nature to him? No. Monica would not play the good daughter for the sake of her father's appearance. So once they were of an age when they were no longer forced to go, Monica and her sister stayed at home while their mother played her part of the fool. Only their brother Jeff went. But he took after his father, and going had never been about the message for him; he went for the women. He never cared about God or what good He could do.

"It's a damn shame when your own children have no faith in what you preach to everyone else," Monica had said to Karen one day.

"I hear you, girl. Just knowing the bullshit that man practices is what keeps my ass at home. Why should I go to his or any other church for that matter, just to listen to a hypocrite?"

Hypocrites.

Her father; who she and her sister called "minister", for being an ordained gigolo.

Her mother; for living a lie, pretending to be happy, when everyone else around them knew that she wasn't.

Hypocrisy.

Monica's life was filled with it. That's why she followed in Karen's footsteps, left North Carolina, and went to school at the University of Maryland. That's why she never moved back home. She wouldn't be forced to be a hypocrite for anybody.

"I really need to go, Mama."

Her mother exhaled. "OK, OK. Fine. Obviously work comes before family, so I'll just do as you wish and make this short and sweet. You've probably forgotten, but my birthday is next month."

"I know, Mama."

"I'm surprised, seeing as how you never remember to call."

Monica held her tongue. She didn't want to get into

anything with her mother. She didn't have the time and more importantly, she didn't have the desire. The last conversation they'd had, Monica had been bold enough to ask why her mother had stayed with a man who never respected her enough to be faithful. Her mother felt the question had been disrespectful. The why hadn't been anyone else's business but hers. After a few minutes of yelling, the conversation ended with both women hanging up the phone, angry about the truth of their words.

"Anyway," her mother continued, "I'm plannin' a birthday dinner for myself, and I want everyone to be there."

"Mama, we should be cooking for you. It's your birthday, after all."

"Exactly girl, which is why I want to cook. Now are you comin' or not?"

"Of course, Mama."

"Make sure you bring Bryce with you."

"I will."

"How is he doing, anyway?"

"He's fine, Mama."

"Good. I look forward to seeing him."

"I'll tell him you said that. Look, Mama . . . I really need to get going," Monica said, looking at her watch.

"OK, OK. Just one more thing."

Monica sighed. "Yes, Mama."

"Don't stress-breath me, girl. I know I raised you with better respect than that."

Monica shook her head. "Sorry, Mama."

"Anyway . . . I just want you to know your father will

be there, and I expect you to respect him. Don't call him the minister. Call him by what he is . . . your daddy. Is that understood?"

Monica mumbled a soft, "Yes Ma'am," and didn't say another word.

"Go on to your meeting, girl. Make sure you and Bryce don't forget about my dinner."

"We won't, Mama."

"OK. I love you, baby."

"I love you too."

Monica hung up the phone, surprised by the tenderness at the end of the call in her mother's voice. For some reason, she had the feeling those three words had meant much more. She raised both eyebrows, then checked her watch again. The conversation had cost her another ten minutes. She grabbed her laptop case and hurried out the door. On the way to her car is when she realized that Bryce hadn't called.

2

Bryce opened his eyes and thought about the dream he'd had. Perhaps nightmare was a better word for it.

He'd just come home from a night out with his brother, Nate, his coworker and major player, Justin, and his soon to be brother-in-law, Alex. They'd gone to the Latin Palace in Baltimore near Fells Point to get their salsa groove on. Alex, the only Latino of the clique, had turned Bryce on to salsa and merengue, when they met three years ago, which is how long Bryce had been dating Monica, who was Alex's sister-in-law. It was Alex's idea to go to the club. Their ladies were having their own night out, so after Alex suggested the place, Bryce called Nate and Justin, and it was on.

Neither Nate nor Justin were hip to salsa, but they couldn't argue the fact that Latin women were beautiful to look at. And for Nate, who was married, looking was about all he could do.

After downing a couple of beers, Bryce and Alex, who refused to be relegated to just looking, danced and twirled with as many Latinas they could find, while Justin ran "mack" lines and practiced what little Spanish he remembered from seventh grade. Nate chilled at the bar. He was determined to stay out of trouble's way.

Nate was a lean, but muscular six foot six, and resembled Michael Jordan; only with a faded beard. He looked more like thirty than his actual thirty-nine, and because women found his looks appealing, chilling by the bar was his best bet. Although he was faithfully married to his high school sweetheart, Felicia, he was still a man, and temptation was a beast.

At thirty, Bryce resembled Nate, only he was six inches shorter, and instead of a shaved dome, he had naturally curly hair kept low and faded at the sides, and unlike his big brother, he didn't have facial hair. "Pretty Rickey" is what most people called him.

Bryce's parents were responsible for his attitude and style. Growing up, he and his brother had never been allowed to leave the house looking any kind of way. Their shoes had to be tied, their pants crisp and held up with a belt, and their shirts ironed and tucked. If they didn't adhere to those rules, then they weren't going anywhere. Bryce never minded the fuss. He'd always liked to look sharp; his father always looked sharp. And as Bryce learned early on, women paid attention to a man who could dress. Unlike his younger brother, Nate never cared about fashion and style. He was a blue-collar kind of guy and he liked the blue-collar style of clothing. While Bryce preferred expensive clothing and designer labels, Nate opted for the clearance section and wore no-name brands. He didn't see the sense in spending an arm and a leg. Nate believed that, contrary to popular belief, the man made the clothes, and not the other way around. And because he never had any problems attracting women, he never spent more than he needed to. But that didn't mean that he couldn't dress. Truth be told, Nate could dress with the best of them. Felicia could testify to that.

It always amused Bryce how his big brother would come out and keep to himself. The only thing Bryce could figure was that after being married for fifteen years, with two kids, going out and chilling with a beer was a much welcomed treat. Bryce knew he would get to that point someday, because he loved Monica, and planned to marry her. That's why he was looking for a ring. But he loved to dance too. And married or not, he would continue to get his groove on. So he did. Until his feet hurt, and the DJ announced that the club was getting ready to close. When that happened, the fellas went their separate ways.

After calling to see if Karen would answer the phone, Alex raced home to beat her there. Although they had a good, solid marriage, Karen was still a woman, and Alex chose peace and tranquility over drama. That's what his father had done, and that's why his parents were still married.

By some miracle, Justin found a way to impress a female and left with her to go back to his bachelor pad for an after-hours fiesta. He and Bryce worked together, so Bryce knew he'd get the dirty details the next day.

Bryce and Nate always traveled together, and because it was better to roll in a Benz than a mini-van, Bryce drove. After dropping Nate off, Bryce went home.

That's when the nightmare began.

Walking in the house, Bryce saw the message light blinking on the answering machine. He figured it had to be from Monica checking up on him. She loved him and trusted him, but she still liked to keep tabs on her man. He smiled. He wasn't bothered by it at all. At least she wasn't psychotic with the checkups like the last woman he'd dated had been. The last thing he wanted to deal with was another every-ten-minute-calling-surprise-visit-springing-jealous-of-the-wind-no-trusting-woman.

Bryce took off his shoes, socks, sweaty shirt, went to the answering machine and hit the playback button. He had only one message.

It wasn't from Monica.

Bryce, this is Nicole. I know it's been a while and I know that I'm the last person you expected to hear from, but there's something that you need to know. Please call me tonight when you get in. I saw you at the Latin Palace. Call me. It's an emergency.

Bryce sighed, shook his head, rose from his bed, and slipped out of his boxers and trudged into the bathroom to shower. He hated to go to bed smelling like sweat. As the water beat down on his tired body, Nicole Anderson danced around in his mind. She'd been a consultant hired to help the financing department work on Renfroe and

Morgan's budget, a software company Bryce had been a programmer for. Fred Morgan, part owner and Bryce's boss, was Nicole's father. Although at the time no one knew that, because Nicole never called Fred, Daddy. He was Mr. Morgan and she'd been the blonde chick named Ms. Anderson. She used her mother's maiden name.

He hadn't intended on it happening, but at some point, Bryce ended up having a sexual no-strings-attached relationship with Nicole on the side, while he dated Monica. It was wrong, but it had been perfect for Bryce. He got to act out his freakiest desires with Nicole, who was only too willing to fulfill his needs, as well as satisfy her own carnal nature; and make sweet, tender love to Monica. He and Nicole met whenever and wherever they could, for as long as they could. Fifteen minute quickies in his office after hours, twenty minute rides in the back of his Durango in any dark parking lot they could find; all day sex-sessions at her place whenever Monica had been away. If they could find the time, they did the crime. But as much as he enjoyed the sexual escapades, he couldn't ignore the fact that he'd truly been in love with Monica and wanted to marry her. Despite Nicole's reluctance, he ended the affair.

That had been four months ago. To his surprise, Nicole kept her mouth shut and didn't seek vengeance by getting Bryce fired. The only thing Bryce could figure was that she didn't want her father to know she'd been getting down and dirty with a Black man, and he was fine with that. He was also okay with the cold shoulder and silent treatment Nicole offered. He was looking forward to marital bliss and Nicole being a non-existent presence in his life was cool with him. So the message on his machine baffled him.

Emergency?

If she'd seen him at the club, why hadn't she approached him?

Although it was nearly three o'clock in the morning, he reluctantly dialed her number when he got out of the shower. When she answered, he didn't know what to say, so he said the only thing he could: "You called?"

Nicole breathed heavily into the receiver. "I'm pregnant."

Bryce pulled the phone away from his ear and stared at it as though the receiver itself had been the one to utter the words.

When he placed it back against his ear, he heard Nicole say, "Bryce . . . are you there? Did you hear what I said?"

Bryce cleared his throat. "I heard you. But why are you telling me this?"

"Because it's yours, Bryce."

Bryce let what she said register for a second. His? Oh hell no! Did she really think he was stupid enough to fall for a line like that? "Look Nicole, I know you're still upset about me ending what we had, but going this route is really not cool."

"Excuse me? You think I'm making this up?"

"Come on Nicole. You and I both know you're not pregnant. Let's not play games here. Now I'm going to bed. And please don't call me anymore. Go and harass the next man because I don't have time for your childish shit." Bryce prepared to hang up the phone, but before he could, Nicole yelled out.

"I'm not playing any games, Bryce. I'm four months pregnant, and it's yours. You do the math!" Before Bryce could respond, the line went dead.

He stood with the receiver glued to his ear.

Pregnant?

Four months?

The math?

He thought back to their last episode together. Monica had been out of town on business, and Bryce had decided that evening, to tell Nicole he wanted to end their fling. They had just come back to her place after going out to dinner and a movie. Remaining outside of her door, Bryce opened his mouth to tell her his decision, but before he could, Nicole wrapped her arms around him, stuck her tongue down his throat, and groped his instantly erect penis. He thought about pulling away from her, but then figured what the hell. One last fuck couldn't hurt. But unlike all of the other times, Bryce hadn't been prepared for the sex. He had no condoms. But again, he thought, what could it hurt?

That had been four months ago.

"Damn!"

Bryce opened and closed his brown eyes again, and rose from his bed. "What a fucking dream," he whispered. He got up to go to the bathroom to take a piss.

That's when he saw the lamp he had busted in his tirade after doing his math.

Bryce quickly forgot all about the bathroom and the pressure on his bladder, and sat back down on the bed.

"Shit."

3

Karen eased out of bed and put her feet down on her plush, almost white carpeting. She hated getting up early on Saturdays but she had no choice. She had to look sharp for Monday because top executives from the TBS Network wanted to meet with her to discuss the possibility of taking her Ladies Holla show national. With the success of the Tyler Perry show, TBS wanted to add daytime talk show to their repertoire. Karen hoped to eventually land a contract with one of the major networks. She wanted to be big like Ellen and Oprah. If the meeting went well, TBS would be her springboard.

She'd always wanted to become a talk show host. As a little girl, she dreamed of being on TV. She wanted to interview people, and make them laugh, cry, and make life-changing decisions the way Phil Donahue had done. Karen always had a mouth and had always been opinionated. Her family called her a natural born talker, and they'd been right. She'd been born with the gift of gab. Undoubtedly, she could talk a car salesman into buying the very same car he was trying to sell to her, and then convince him that having the vehicle would help boost his sales. She'd make him get the warranty too.

A natural born talker.

That was the one trait Karen got from her father, who she hadn't spoken to in almost a year. Karen's father, the good minister. At least that's what the people who didn't know the real man behind the cloth thought. For those who had known him, he'd been a smooth-talking-breast-and-ass-seeking pastor, who could deliver God's word and make the devil himself, feel the spirit. Karen never took to heart any of her father's words. From the time she was small, she and her sister had known their father to be a hypocrite. He'd been a womanizer to the nth degree, and their brother, Jeff, had been just like him.

The contempt Karen felt toward her father also affected her relationship with her mother. Like Monica, Karen had trouble accepting the fact that her mother allowed herself to be disrespected the way she had been. She never could understand why her mother put up with her father's roving ways. Because of the lack of respect Karen felt, she never developed a close relationship with her mother.

She grew up unable to avoid the stares or hearing the whispers about "Those poor children and the spineless wife."

Because her father and his exploits had been so well known, Karen left North Carolina after she graduated from high school and went to the University of Maryland. She wanted to be in a place where no one knew her or had heard of her father. She was glad Monica followed in her footsteps.

Turned off by the example their mother had set, they relied on each other for the strength and determination of never settling when it came to men. Their mother had fallen victim to the life the minister had provided. In Karen's eyes, she'd sold her soul to the devil. Karen would be damned if she did the same. The last thing she was ever going to do was depend on a man for happiness or material things. Even if that man happened to be the one of her dreams.

She looked over at her husband, Alex, as he slept quietly. They'd met at the Latin carnival in Miami four years ago. She hadn't yet had her show and was wasting her mass media degree as a procurement supervisor for Blue Shield. The trip to Miami was supposed to have been her last chance to splurge and vacation, because after the trip, she planned to quit her job and go after her dream. She went with Monica and Maria, her long-time friend from Peru. Although she never listened to Latin music religiously, and didn't understand a word of the language, she always found the rhythm appealing, the singing filled with passion, and the men delicious to look at. That's why she went. For fun and pleasure before the hard work back at home would begin.

She never intended on falling in love.

Especially with Alex.

She'd been in line trying to figure out why the vendor had to have the menu in Spanish, when Alex did the smoothest thing any man had ever done for her and ordered her food, paid for it, and ushered her out of the line without ever asking for her name. Alex was take charge and she liked that. The fact that he could have given Julio and Enrique Iglesias a run for their money in the looks category didn't hurt either. Karen and Alex ended up forgetting that they hadn't gone to the festival alone, and spent the rest of the day getting to know each other. Ironically, they both lived in Maryland, and before they went their separate ways, they exchanged numbers. They were married a year later.

Alex was the perfect man for Karen. He was supportive, yet not afraid to disagree because he had his own mind. He was attentive and knew when to cuddle and when to give her space. He expected the same from her. His love was passionate and total, and he made Karen feel as though there was no other woman in the world for him, not just with words, but with actions as well. Karen adored that feeling and craved his love and affection. In her heart, she knew Alex would never hurt her or be anything like her father. That's why she'd given all of herself to him, and that's why she was anxious to have his child.

Just like Mariah.

Mariah Ortiz.

She was the only glitch in what would have otherwise been a perfect world. She was Alex's ex with whom he had a child. Perhaps ex was too strong of a word.

Mistake.

That was a better word because that's exactly what Mariah had been. A slip-up. An error in judgment. Alex had fallen victim to being a horny, young man who'd been caught up by a pretty face and a smile. Their brief moment of passion produced Miguel, an angel of a son who thankfully looked like his father and acted more like him too.

Karen adored Miguel. When Alex first told her that he had a son, she'd been immediately apprehensive about getting involved with him. Baby Mama Drama–she'd seen and heard too much of it to want to get involved. She didn't want to have to deal with exes and their jealous, manipulative, conniving, bitching ways. And that's what Alex warned her she'd be dealing with. And he'd been right.

After making the decision to go forward with Alex, Karen got to see just how much of a bitch Mariah was. They'd been officially dating for five months when Karen went with Alex to pick up his son. Still a toddler at three, Alex was going to take him and Karen over to his parents' house to spend the day and have dinner. Miguel was a regular, but this was going to be Karen's first time meeting the family.

The moment Mariah opened the door, she looked over toward Karen, who'd been waiting in the car, and then glared at her baby's father. "*Quien es ella?*"

Alex expected her attitude. "She's my girlfriend."

Karen, who'd kept her window down so she could hear what was being said, smiled proudly.

"Well I don't want her near my son," Mariah countered.

Alex took a deep breath. "He's my son too, Mariah, and you're going to have to get used to seeing Karen. *Ya muevete.*"

Karen didn't know what that meant, but whatever its meaning, she liked it because Alex stormed past Mariah, gathered his son and his things, and came back outside. "We'll all be back later," he said, walking to the car with the cutest little boy Karen had ever seen.

Unfortunately, Mariah's tirade wasn't over. She rushed behind him. "Don't think I'm going to let you get away with this, *sucio. Miguel es mi hijo.* And I don't want him near that bitch. *Una Negra fea!* You should be ashamed of yourself."

Karen, who heard the word bitch and surmised that *Negra* could only mean one thing, got out of the car. "Look," she said, determined to keep her cool more for the baby's sake than anything, "why don't you just let us go and keep your son from having to witness this spectacle."

"Excuse me?" Mariah said, her tone bitter. "But this is none of your fucking business."

Karen clenched her jaws. "Listen, we don't know each other, so there's no need for you and me to argue. Besides, I don't think you really want your neighbors to hear and see all of this."

Mariah slit her eyes and stiffened her neck. "*No me importa que tu piensas! No me hablas de mi hijo. Puta negra!*"

As much as she tried not to, Karen reached her boiling point. "Okay . . . You've used that word one too many times." She stepped forward intending on doing some damage, but luckily for Mariah, Alex stepped in front of her.

"Karen, can you take Miguel and put him in his car seat for me, please?" he asked locking his eyes with hers.

Karen looked at Mariah, then at Alex. "If you weren't the one," she said, kissing him for Mariah to see. Then she took Miguel, who smiled and cooed. As she buckled him into the seat, she smiled as Alex went off in Spanish to Mariah. Mariah then stormed into her house and slammed the door behind her. When Alex got in the car, he shook his head.

"I'm sorry about that."

Karen hmph'd. "Don't be sorry. Just be glad you stepped in when you did."

Alex laughed. "Did you really mean what you said about me being the one?"

Karen gave a devilish smile, licked her lips, and leaned towards him. "I meant it."

And she had.

Alex was her man, her soulmate. Too bad her mother couldn't understand that. When she first told her mother of her engagement to Alex, her mother didn't speak.

After a few minutes, her mother said, "I didn't raise you to be with someone outside of your race, chile."

"But Mama, this is love. This is bigger than race."

"Not to me it isn't. Not to my own mama who was killed by little White devils. Not to my daddy who was beaten by the Klan!"

"Alex isn't white, Mama."

"Chile, his skin is light and his hair ain't like your daddy's. He's closer to them than we are."

"You haven't even met him yet."

"And I don't want to. Black is what you are, and black is where you belong. Chile, when your daddy finds out—"

"I don't give a damn what *he* thinks. His feelings are

the last ones I'm concerned with. I can't believe after all he's done, you still care about what he feels."

"He is my husband and your daddy! I'm tired of tellin' you and your sister to respect that. And don't you ever use such language with me again. I am your mama and I will *still* whup your behind. Now I'm sorry that you dislike the fact that I don't approve of your future husband, but that's just the way it is."

Karen sighed and fought the tears that welled in her eyes. She may not have agreed with the things her mother did, but she was still her mother regardless and she wanted her to be happy for her.

Karen and Alex had a small wedding consisting of a few close friends and family. Jeff and a few cousins came, and Monica was the maid of honor. Her parents never came.

Despite the absence of her parents, Karen was still happy. Alex became her husband, and that's all that mattered. Karen's parents didn't meet Alex until two years after they were married. Her father had a special sermon to give in a church in downtown Baltimore, and had it not been for that, Karen doubted the meeting would have ever occurred.

Karen leaned over and kissed Alex gently on his forehead. He never stirred. She was anxious to break the news about the pregnancy to him. She'd been looking forward to sharing the experience with him and his family, whom she'd grown very close to. Although she was never in competition with her, Mariah would no longer be able to say that she had something of Alex's that she didn't.

Karen rose from the bed and was on her way to the bathroom when the phone rang. She hurried to pick it up before it could wake Alex. "Hello?" she said softly.

"Good morning, chile."

Karen raised an eyebrow. "Mama?"

"Why you sound so surprised to hear from me? I ain't dead yet."

"It's . . . it's been a while, Mama."

"More your fault than mine, chile," her mother said. "Anyway . . . how is Alex?"

Karen didn't answer right away as shock came over her. She'd asked about Alex? "He's fine," she said finally.

"Is he awake?"

"N . . . no."

"Well tell him I said hello when he wakes up."

"I will," Karen said. She didn't know what to make of her mother's pleasantries toward Alex. "Is everything okay, Mama?"

"Everything is fine, chile."

"OK."

"You have a minute, or are you as busy as your sister?"

"I'm actually getting ready to get dressed. I have a hair appointment that I need to get to."

"You and your sister . . . I'll make this quick then. My birthday is next month and I'm going to cook a birthday dinner to celebrate. I want you and Alex to be there."

"Huh?" Karen said shocked.

"I said–"

"I heard what you said, Mama. I'm just having trouble with what you said."

"I'm cooking dinner for my birthday and I want you and Alex there. What is it you're having trouble with?"

"You want Alex there?"

"Yes."

"Are you sure you're okay, Mama?"

"I told you I'm fine. Now . . . are you two comin' or not?"

"Y . . . yes. Of course we'll come."

"Good. You need the address?"

"Of course not, Mama."

"Just checking, seeing as how you and your sister seem to have forgotten all about us over here."

"We haven't forgotten you guys, Mama. We're just both busy."

"Too busy to call your mama for four months?"

"Mama . . ."

"Go and run to your hair appointment, chile. We'll speak when you come for dinner."

Karen sighed. "Okay, Mama. It . . . it was good to hear from you."

"It was good to talk to you, baby. I love you."

"I love you too, Mama."

Karen hung up the phone and didn't move for a few seconds. She was in shock. Her mother wanted to celebrate her birthday and she wanted Alex there. This had been the first time she'd ever used Alex's name in a positive manner. She'd said that she was fine, but Karen had trouble accepting that.

What was behind the dinner?

4

Alex turned on the stereo and put in his new Grupo Niche CD. He couldn't carry a tune to save his life, but he sang right along with the song regardless and proceeded to make up the bed. This was something he had learned to do since marrying Karen three years ago. He remembered the first time she fussed over the bed not being made. They'd just moved in together, after deciding to do the let-me-see-if-I-can-live-with-you-and-accept-your-nasty- habits-before-I-marry-you trial run. After a morning bout of lovemaking, Karen showered and left for work, leaving Alex completely spent in the bed. A network operations manager, he was working the third shift again that week, and didn't have to be in until 7:00 PM. Although she had one of the highest rated talk shows in the DC, Baltimore area, Karen's Ladies Holla show hadn't soared to great heights yet. So while she hustled to make the show a success, Alex slept and dreamt, waking up for only a few hours to eat and watch Karen's live show before going back to dreamland.

By the time he woke up, it was five o'clock and time for him to get up and get ready for his forty-five minute commute to work. Karen, who always spent hours going over the pros and cons of the day's production, and then prepared for the next day's taping, never got home until after Alex had long gone.

When Alex finally left, he'd made the near-fatal mistake of not making up the bed. He never heard the end of it when he got home. One of Karen's pet peeves was a messy bed. She believed in her mother's old philosophy that a messy bed made for a messy life. She couldn't stand seeing rumpled sheets, and she always made sure to make the bed before she left for work. When Alex walked into the bedroom after a frustrating night of work, Karen didn't hesitate to tell him how inconsiderate he'd been by "sleeping all damn day and not making up the bed."

Had she taken things too far?

Of course she had.

Alex, as tired as he was, laughed at her tirade. Karen, of course, didn't find it as amusing as he had, and when he mocked her, it only added fuel to her fire.

Alex chuckled to himself as he fluffed the pillows. That first, and only night of complaints over the bed, had been a memorable one in more ways than one because right after Karen finished nagging, they made love as though it were going to be their last time. Arguments and sex always made for an exciting morning of passion.

After smoothing out the sheets, Alex moved to the bathroom to brush his teeth, shower, and shave. He'd taken the Saturday off because he'd promised Miguel he would take him to the park to play basketball. With seven years of age behind him, Miguel was the spitting image of Alex, in both attitude and look. He had the same intense light green eyes, the same bubble nose, and full lips, and along with those lady-killer looks, Miguel also had Alex's stubborn attitude. He was also a competitor like his father. Playing basketball that day had been Miguel's decision because he wanted desperately to beat his father.

While Alex scrubbed away plaque and morning funk, he smiled. His son's tenacity always made him proud. Miguel's determination made Alex think of his days as a young son unable to beat his father in basketball. No matter how hard he tried, sweated and hustled, Alex's father never gave him the pleasure of tasting anything but the sour taste of defeat. Alex was eighteen when he finally won a game of thirty-three. The moment the ball sighed through the net, he knew that the victory had been his father's way of saying welcome to manhood. Alex hopped into the shower. Miguel had a long way to go before becoming a man.

He was glad that the only trait Miguel had gotten from his mother had been curly hair. Although he cherished his son, and didn't regret for a second the day he was born, he wouldn't have minded if he had come from some other woman's womb.

Mariah Ortiz.

Miguel's mother.

Alex's nightmare.

He was twenty-three and working as a manager in *The Wall* music store when Mariah walked into his life, bringing with her a route that he would never be able to turn away from. With a Jennifer Lopez body, long curly brown hair that looked permanently wet, and feline eyes that could hypnotize a priest into committing sin, Alex had damn near exploded in his khakis when she walked into the store requesting an application for employment. Mariah was all Latina, and Alex didn't hesitate to hire her on the spot.

Ignoring the company's strict policy forbidding the dating of employees, Alex pursued Mariah for two months before finally getting her to agree to go out with him. It would only take that one date for his life to forever be changed. So caught up by her body and innocent smile, Alex did the one thing he swore he would never do—had unprotected sex. In the back of his father's Chevrolet Cavalier no less!

Four weeks later, Mariah came to him and told him she'd just failed a pregnancy test.

When Mariah initially dropped the news on him, he had been speechless. He wanted to be angry with her, but he knew that the only person he could have truly been angry with was himself. He let the wrong head do the thinking for him, and he'd paid the price. He wasn't ready to be a father, but what could he do?

Although he never suggested it, Mariah let him know very quickly that she wasn't going to have an abortion, which was fine with him, because that was something that neither he nor his family believed in. His mother and father always raised him to face any and all responsibilities head on.

"You reap what you sow," his father would tell him and his three older brothers. "Life is a game, and if you're going to play, you better be ready to deal with whatever pops up."

So that's exactly what Alex did.

He grew up and dealt with having to be a father. Life was no longer just his own to toy with. He had a baby on the way, and the baby's mother, he quickly realized, he could not stand.

Look up the word bitch in the dictionary, and Mariah's picture is what you'd find—at least that's how Alex felt.

The only thing she and Alex had in common was the sex, which produced Miguel. Other than that, they were at the opposite ends of the personality spectrum. Although Alex had his rough side, he was for the most part a gentle and sensitive man. He didn't mind doing for others and getting nothing in return. Alex had been taught the value of generosity and selflessness from his parents. He was raised with a belief in Christ, and that through Him all things were possible. His mother, who had won the Miss Puerto Rico pageant when she was younger, never let Alex, or his brothers, Carlos, Julio, and Marco, skip church on Sundays. Getting Alex's father to go had been impossible, and so she didn't try. It's not that he didn't believe in God, or have faith. He simply had too much soccer to watch on Sundays.

Alex's father was a stern disciplinarian. School came before anything else. He was determined to have his sons succeed and take advantage of the opportunities he never had. That's why he moved them from Puerto Rico to Maryland. Although he was rough and overly demanding at times, his strict ways paid off. All four sons went to college. Alex entered the telecommunication field, Marco became an accountant, the oldest, Carlos, became a pediatrician, and Julio started his own record production company.

Alex loved both his mother and father equally, and after watching them for all of his twenty-three years, he hoped to be as lucky as they were some day. For Alex, taking on the responsibility of a child was a joy to be cherished.

For Mariah, however, it was the complete opposite. Mariah wasn't raised with the same type of love Alex was. Although born in Puerto Rico, her mother, Lyda, became a child of the streets of New York at an early age. After giving birth to Mariah at age fifteen, those very same streets became Mariah's surrogate parents. She never knew her father, and her mother had been too irresponsible and immature to make her daughter her number one priority. So, Mariah learned all about life and how to survive it from what she witnessed and experienced day after day in the Bronx.

She grew up hard and grew up fast. By the age of ten she was routinely getting drunk and high. By twelve, sex was as common to her as taking a bath. When she was fourteen she had her first child, Christina, a secret that very few people knew about. Because both she and her mother, who by that time had devoted her life to crack, were financially unable to care for the baby, Mariah's aunt, Lyda's sister, who had been visiting from Puerto Rico, took Christina back with her to raise the innocent child as her own. Mariah never protested, because she hadn't wanted the responsibility anyway, and her mother had been too high to care that she wouldn't see her granddaughter.

After Christina's birth, Mariah got on birth control and was fine until her mother died of an overdose a couple of months before Mariah's sixteenth birthday. Mariah never shed a tear. With no parent, she hustled on the streets and prostituted herself for money, food, and clothing. It was during this time she ran into one of her mother's ex-boyfriends, Omar. Back in the day, Omar, who used to get high with Lyda, had been the closest thing to a father that Mariah had ever known. He dated Lyda for almost two years and was the only man who tried to get her to quit drugs, but it didn't work. And after she cursed him out and let him know that he was no longer needed, Omar left New York to live with his brother in Baltimore. There he got himself cleaned up, got a job, and eventually a wife. Despite being constantly strung out, Omar had loved Lyda and cared for Mariah, and regarded her as his adoptive daughter of sorts. So after finding out about Lyda's death, he traveled back to New York to find out what happened to the little girl he had never forgotten. It was on the street where he found her. Mariah, dirty, skinny, and starving, didn't recognize Omar, and approached him, offering to give him a blow job in exchange for money. Without fail, and because she had been too weak to resist, Omar took Mariah back with him to Baltimore.

She lived there with him and his wife, a White woman

with Mrs. Brady's personality, and attended high school. Because she had never been forced to take school seriously, Mariah managed to get her high school diploma, but had no plans for college. Omar, knowing how rough her life had been, allowed her to follow her own path. All he demanded was that if she didn't go to school, then she would work and help pay the phone and electric bills. So with limited skills, she went to the mall to find a job.

She met Alex when she was nineteen, and she didn't intentionally set out to get pregnant—it just happened. Mariah never really liked Alex; she just found him cute. Plus he drove a nice car. She went out with him because he had given her a job when no one else would. Having sex was just routine. Although, Omar had taken her from the streets and given her a better life, the streets never left Mariah, and just as she did in the past, she used sex to get her what she wanted. She wanted a raise—sex would get her that. So she fucked Alex. And that's all it was—a fuck. He wasn't supposed to stay inside of her. All of the guys she'd slept with, who'd gone bareback, had been smart enough to pull out before their explosion.

But not Alex.

He came, and came hard. And her life was forever changed.

Mariah loved her son, but just couldn't get past the feeling that his existence was a burden to her. Omar and his wife were great in the beginning, but once he got past the terrible two phase, they made sure that Mariah understood Miguel was her responsibility. She knew that her son was a beautiful and special gift from God, but no matter how hard she tried not to let it bother her, she couldn't stand the fact that the older he got, the more he acted like his father. And she couldn't stand Alex. Had Miguel never entered into the equation, that brief moment of sex would have been the only thing they ever would have shared. Now they were linked for life.

Alex dressed and shook his head at his predicament. He had a son with a woman he despised, and was married to Karen, who accepted and loved Miguel, and barely tolerated Mariah, who never hesitated to get on Karen's last nerve.

From the very beginning, Alex made sure Karen knew about Miguel and his strained relationship with Mariah. At first Karen had been apprehensive about getting involved with Alex, but eventually the apprehension went away. They dated for six months before Alex proposed. In Karen, he'd found the woman with whom he could be married to for years and always be satisfied.

Alex laced up his Jordan sneakers and slipped into his Washington Wizards jersey—number twenty-three, of course. He was anxious to see his son, but not in the mood to deal with Mariah's bullshit.

5

"I want to change my life man, but I don't know how."

"Huh?"

Jeff looked at his friend, Gregg, for a moment before taking a shot at the basket. "I love women, Gregg. I can't get enough of them."

"And that's a problem?"

Jeff sighed. "For me it is."

"What are you . . . gay?"

Jeff gave Gregg a hard chest pass. "Shut up, man! No, I'm not gay. I'm just saying, I need to make a change."

"I don't get it."

"My father was a womanizing son of a bitch, man. Shit . . . he probably still is, even at sixty-five."

"Your father's the man," Gregg said with a smile.

Jeff shook his head. "No . . . he's not. He never has been. And I've followed in his footsteps."

"Man . . . you've completely lost me."

Jeff took a pass from Gregg, took two dribbles, and then hopped off his left foot and took the ball in for a smooth finger roll layup. He caught the ball as it fell through the net and then went and sat down on the ground, leaning back against the fence. It was a warm seventy degrees.

Gregg came and sat down beside him, sipping from a water bottle. "You okay, man?"

Jeff sighed. "You know . . . this thing I have going with Sherry . . . it's good, man."

Gregg nodded. "Yes it is. So what's problem?"

"I don't know, man. I guess I'm just worried that I'll fuck it up."

"What do you mean?"

"I love women, man."

Gregg chuckled. "Don't we all?"

Jeff shook his head. "No man, I mean I really love them. Their smiles, their eyes, their bodies, their scents. I love being with women, man. And I know them. I know what they want, what they like, need, deserve—what they crave. I know what they want to hear. I know women, man."

Gregg laughed. "Sounds like you need to write a book, man."

Jeff frowned. His father had been a master with women. He'd watched and studied him as he grew up. He sat in pews with his Bible in his lap, and admired how the women in the congregation stared at his father with fiery lust in their eyes. He watched him work them over; manipulate them with slick smiles, subtle glances, and holy words. Jeff watched, studied, soaked in the lessons daily and now at twenty-five, Jeff was the man the women wanted and admired.

Just as his father had been, he'd become the "catch". Handsome, with his father's broad shoulders, strong jaw-line, and deep, velvet tone. Inviting, with his mother's dark-brown skin, brown, deep-set eyes, and disarmingly seductive smile. Educated, with a Ph.D. in psychology from the University of North Carolina. Successful, with his own private practice in Charlotte, a fancy house with a Porsche in the garage, and a Hummer he drove daily.

Women could never get enough of him. They'd always liked to drink him in as though he were a refreshing cup of hot chocolate to warm their cold souls.

He should have been happy. He was living every man's fantasy. He had the job, cars, money, home, and even better, no kids or baby mama drama.

He should have been happy.

But he was scared.

For the first time ever, he'd found a woman that stirred him well beyond just making his dick hard. Sherry McCann. He'd been seeing her for four months. Sherry resembled Demi Moore with long, straight brown hair. At five foot nine, she was two inches shorter than Jeff, so when they spoke, they were nearly eye-to-eye, which signified no real dominance for him—something he'd always been accustomed to. Like him, Sherry had no kids. Her career as a criminal prosecutor was her top priority. Jeff liked the drive in her. He loved her professional style, her sharp mind. She was precisely the type of woman he'd always wanted. The type of woman he could see himself settling down with.

And that scared him.

He'd spent so much of his life mirroring his father's

ways that as he fell more and more in love with Sherry, he began to wonder if he'd be able to commit in a way he, nor his father ever had. He didn't want to do to Sherry what his father had done to his mother. He didn't want to be that type of man. But he was around women all the time, and try as he might, he could never seem to quiet a grumbling inside of him when they were around.

"Sometimes, man," he said, tapping the ball with the tip of his index finger, "sometimes I just want to head to the jewelry store, buy a ring, and then head over to Sherry's and drop down on one knee and pop the question."

"And other times?"

"Other times . . . other times I just want to tap the next piece of fine ass that I see."

Gregg couldn't help it. He laughed again. "Well . . . I'm not married and I'm not attached, so you know how I feel about tapping fine ass."

"Being single isn't all it's cracked up to be, man. It can't touch having the right woman by your side."

"So if you feel like you have the right woman, what's the problem?"

Jeff frowned again and shrugged his shoulders. "I don't know, man. I guess I just really don't want to follow in my father's footsteps. On one hand, I really respect him, but on another, I have none for him."

Gregg hmph'd. "Sounds to me like you're gonna have to have a real pow wow with yourself."

"I have been, Gregg. Every day."

"You ever try to talk to your mother about it? You know . . . get her perspective without coming out and saying, 'Mom . . . how do I not be a womanizer like Dad was?'"

Jeff took a breath and exhaled slowly. "Nah . . . we're not close like that."

"Yeah? How come?"

"My mother grew up in the South during a time when Blacks had to struggle to gain respect. When she was a kid, her mother was murdered by four teenage white boys. Ever since then, she's had ill feelings toward Whites. I've dated more white women than anything. It's not something I've consciously done. That's just who I've been attracted to. Because of that, my mother and I . . . we just never really got close. I know things were hard back then, but it's a different time now. I know racism is still alive and ticking, but the world has changed. I mean, shit, we have a black president, and it's because white people helped put him there."

"Does she know about Sherry?"

Jeff shook his head. "Nah, I would love to talk to her about Sherry, but my mother's set in her ways. Sad thing is, I think my mother would really dig her. Sherry might not be black, but she has a feistiness that I think my mother would appreciate."

"What about your dad? Does he have a problem with Whites?"

"Shit . . . my dad could care less about color. 'Pussy has no face' . . . that's something he told me a long time ago."

Gregg laughed. "Wise words, my friend. Wise words."

"Whatever, man," Jeff said, laughing.

"So what are you gonna do? Move forward with Sherry? Pull back?"

Jeff shrugged and then rose from the ground. "I don't know for sure, man, but, honestly, pulling back just doesn't seem like an option to me."

"So basically, you need to stop being a bitch and head on over to the jewelry store and cop that ring."

"I guess so." Jeff took a few dribbles to the free throw line, turned, and took a quick turn-around jumper, swishing the ball through the net. "Enough talking, man. I want to go for three in a row."

Gregg stood up. "Whatever, man. Just check the damn ball."

Jeff laughed, knowing another victory was on the way.

Later that evening, he stood at the head of his oak dining table set for two and smiled. He had hooked it up. China plates, sterling silver knife and fork set with gold tips, pearl white cloth napkins folded into precise triangles. To complete the setting, crystal champagne glasses eagerly awaited the Merlot wine he had sitting in the refrigerator. Two candles sat in the middle of the table, while a dozen red long-stemmed roses lay on the chair that Sherry would be sitting in when she came over.

He took a deep breath through his nostrils. The baked chicken would be done soon. He'd already prepared the dirty rice with olives, kidney beans with small chunks of potatoes, and sweet corn. He was excited. After his talk with Gregg on the basketball court, he did exactly what his friend suggested, and headed to the jewelry store and bought a diamond engagement ring. He was still scared, but he knew letting Sherry go wasn't an option.

He walked into the kitchen and turned off the oven. He'd never had to cook when he was younger. The kitchen had usually been reserved for his mother and sisters, while he and his father took care of the "manly" duties. Jeff had been renting a studio apartment during his second year at UNC when he taught himself how to cook. Always a ladies man, he realized early on that the best way to impress a woman and get her clothes off was through her stomach. See, women had it backward. They assumed that to get to a man's heart they had to know their way around the kitchen, but Jeff knew better. While a man appreciated good cooking, in all actuality, they didn't really care about the food. Hell, a man would eat for weeks on fast food if the ass was tight, breasts ample, and pussy sweet. That was what was important to a man.

But a woman . . .

They were impressed by a man who wasn't afraid of the kitchen. A man slaving away with pots and pans made them weak in the knees, and guaranteed sex. So he didn't just learn how to cook. He learned how to Cook with a capital C. Southern, French, Spanish, Caribbean, Chinese, Italian—he could Cook them all. With the help of cookbooks and cooking channels, Jeff learned all about the different spices, seasonings, and oils. He studied the art of marinating, tenderizing, and accessorizing. Jeff learned how to cook, and the women loved him for it, and thanked him by doing things in bed that would give their mothers heart attacks and send their fathers searching for the shotgun.

He checked the time displayed on the microwave—ten minutes to eight. Sherry would be arriving soon. She had a late meeting with a client. He poured himself a glass of wine and was about to go and relax in the living room when the phone rang. Hopefully it wasn't Sherry calling to say she needed more time because the closer the time came to Sherry arriving, the harder his heart beat.

He answered the phone. "Hello?"

"Hello, Jeffrey."

"Mama?"

"How are you?"

"I'm good, Mama."

"Are you busy?"

"A little."

"Let me guess, I caught you at a bad time too," his mother said.

"Unfortunately . . . yeah. I have company coming over soon."

"I see. Would that be a lady friend?"

"Yes," Jeff answered apprehensively. He clenched his jaws and waited for the next question that she always asked: "Is she another White woman?"

But it never came. Instead his mother asked, "Is she a nice woman?"

Jeff raised his left eyebrow. "I'm sorry, what did you say, Mama?"

"I asked if she was a nice woman."

"Y . . . Yes she is," Jeff stammered, not sure how to take her question.

"What's her name?"

Here we go, Jeff thought. Next, she'd be asking what race she was. "Sherry," he said.

"That's a nice name."

Jeff raised both of his eyebrows at her response, but still waited for the next question.

"So what does Sherry do?" his mother asked sounding genuinely interested.

Jeff didn't answer right away. This wasn't in the script he'd become used to. And it was throwing him off. Something wasn't right. "She's uh . . . she's a lawyer," he finally said.

"That's nice. Have you been dating her long?"

"For a few months now. Mama, are you okay?" Jeff asked.

"Yes . . . I am."

"Is Dad okay?"

"Your father is fine as always. Still speaking the word. But you should know how he is since you speak to him."

Jeff raised his eyebrows again. His mother's comment surprised him. He looked at the clock again. He wanted to get off quickly because he could feel a storm coming. "Mama, I don't mean to rush but . . ."

"I know, I know. You have to get going. I tell you, my children just don't seem to have any time for me. That's all right though. You wait and see, you may just miss me one day."

Jeff opened his mouth to respond, but instead, decided not to say anything. Sherry was coming and he didn't want to be in a bad mood when she arrived.

"Anyway," his mother said, "Before you run off, I just want to tell you that I'm cooking a birthday dinner for myself, and I've invited your sisters and their mates, and I'm inviting you. And if this *friend* of yours is important to you, you can bring her too."

"Excuse me?"

"I'm inviting you and your friend over for my birthday dinner next month. Will you be coming?"

Jeff was speechless, and for a moment wondered if it truly had been his mother he'd been talking to. She was inviting him and Sherry over for dinner? "Mama . . . you do know that Sherry is white, don't you."

His mother sighed. "I assumed so."

"And you want us over for dinner?"

"Yes. Now will you be coming?"

"Y . . . yes . . . I'll . . . I mean we'll come."

"Good. Be on time. Six o'clock."

"OK."

"Goodbye Jeffery. I love you."

"Goodbye, Mama. Love you too."

Jeff's mother hung up the phone, leaving him standing frozen in stunned silence. Invited? Both of them? Something was up. He didn't know what, but he knew it was something.

He checked the time and then went into the kitchen to look at the baking chicken. He was going to pop the question, and his mother had invited him over for dinner and told him to bring Sherry. Was the world coming to an end?

6

Jean sat still on her bed and took a deep breath.

The stage had been set. In one month, she would break the news to her family; while at the same time begin the process of mending wounds before her time was over.

For the first time, since receiving the news, she admitted to herself that she didn't want to die. Especially now that she was ready to take the necessary steps to live a life that she should have been living. A life filled with love, warmth, joy, and true happiness.

The dinner would be a new beginning to an eventual ending, and as that fact sucked air from her chest, tears of pain, sadness, regret, and joy fell from her eyes.

She thought about the death of her mother, something she vaguely remembered. And the death of her father, when she was eighteen. It had been a sad day, but in some respects, it had also been one filled with relief, because for as long as she could remember, her father had always seemed to have a cloud of sadness over him. He'd looked so peaceful the day of his viewing. That was an image she'd always kept with her. Sitting in her chair, she wondered if she would look the same to her children when her time came.

Jean's body trembled as the tears fell harder.

She'd put up with so much for so long. Accepting her husband's philandering ways had done much more than just hurt her emotionally. It had also hurt her relationship with Karen, Monica, and Jeffery. Her daughters didn't speak to her much and she knew why. They didn't respect her. They'd never said that to her, but she could see it in their eyes and hear it in their voice. As for her son . . . he was too much like his father and he sought comfort with white women only. She'd never been privy to a long life with her mother, having lost her at age three, but she missed her, and she could never seem to live without blaming all for acts committed by only a few. Her son wasn't bad or wrong for loving outside of her race, nor was Karen.

Leukemia.

Sad, that it was with only a few months left that she could admit that freely. It was also sad that she had finally decided enough had been enough when it came to Stewart.

"Jean?"

Jean looked up. Stewart was standing in the doorway watching her. Jean hurried to wipe the tears away from her face and cleared her throat. "Yes, Stewart?"

Stewart stepped into the room. "Is everything alright?"

Jean looked at her husband. He was still strikingly

handsome. It wasn't hard for her to see how any woman would be attracted to him. Jean had fallen for him hard, just as all the women had back in their youth. When he chose her to be his, she'd felt blessed. Stewart had been the "chosen one" at that time. Young, confident, sexy, a minister's son with nothing but blessings and good faith bestowed upon him. All of the women wanted to be his. Jean had been no different.

She loved his passion and yearning for the word and teachings of Christ. She loved his spirit and his desire to spread the gospel to others. She was as entranced as everyone else had been when he spoke. He had a charisma that wooed, grabbed tight, and refused to let go. He had a charm that had been, and still was, magnetic.

Their courtship had been a quick one. Within six months of dating, they were married, and six months after that, Jean was pregnant with Karen.

Jean loved Stewart. And she believed that he loved her. He was just a weak man. Something she came to realize early into their marriage. Stewart could not resist the flesh of other women. Jean thought of leaving him once, but that thought quickly disappeared. She'd made a vow before God and for better or worse, she would stand by that vow, no matter how painful and embarrassing his extramarital affairs—affairs that most everyone knew about—had been to endure. Besides, they had children, and there'd been enough loud whispering behind her back about Stewart. The last thing she wanted to have to deal with was people talking about her leaving her husband as well.

So Jean endured.

For years.

But things were different now.

"Everything is fine, Stewart," she said easily.

"You're crying."

"Yes."

"Why?"

Jean opened her mouth. She wanted to tell him that she'd been crying because of everything he'd put her through. That his weakness for the flesh affected not only her spirit, but the spirits of their children as well. She wanted to tell him that she was dying. Instead she lay on her side and said, "I have a headache, Stewart. I'm going to lie down for a while."

"Do you want me to get you anything?"

Jean shook her head. "No."

Stewart nodded, and then said, "I'm going to step out for a while. Mrs. Carter called me earlier. She needs counseling about her daughter. I shouldn't be gone too long."

Jean nodded. "OK."

"Do you want me to get anything while I'm out?"

"No."

"OK." Stewart turned and headed to the door, but paused before leaving the room. "Jean?"

"Yes Stewart?"

"What's the significance of this dinner you're planning?"

"It's my birthday, Stewart. People celebrate birthdays this way."

"I understand that, Jean. I just can't help but wonder why this particular birthday? It's not as though you're celebrating your fiftieth."

"Do I need a specific number to celebrate?"

"No. But you've never been one for a party."

Jean looked over her shoulder at her husband. "It's just time for a change, Stewart. I wanted this birthday to reflect that."

"What do you mean by 'it's time for a change'?"

Jean sighed softly. *Soon,* she thought. *Soon you'll know.* "Tell Carla I said hello, Stewart. I'm going to take a nap now."

Stewart nodded and without saying another word, walked out of the room.

As he did, tears ran down from the corners of Jean's eyes, to the pillow beneath her. Soon, she thought again. Soon.

7

Bryce parked his car and ran his hand through his hair and flared his nostrils while exhaling heavily. It had been a rough day. All day long, thoughts of Nicole and her possible pregnancy had run through his mind and consumed him so much that he had barely gotten anything done. He sat in his office, and for the most part, stared at a picture of him and Monica sitting on his desk. The picture had been taken in the Bahamas. They were there the previous summer for a week-long vacation. It was one of the best times they'd ever had. Fun, sun, and a lot of sex.

Pregnant.

Bryce tried to keep the thoughts out of his mind when he went by Monica's after work. She wanted to celebrate. The Redskins' owner agreed that his team and McMillan and Weber were a perfect fit. With glasses of champagne sitting beside them, Monica and Bryce relaxed in the bathtub. The mood had been romantic. Teddy Pendergrass's hit "Come and Go with Me" sighed softly from the stereo in the living room. Sweet aroma from vanilla scented candles, lit and sitting around the edges of the tub, filled the air. Monica was wet, and it hadn't been just from the water in the tub. She was feeling good and she wanted her man. She always did. She loved to feel his arms wrapped around her in a tight embrace. Especially when they made love in the tub, as they had done many times before.

As Teddy crooned, Monica laid her head back against Bryce's chest and moaned seductively, letting him know what type of mood she was in. On any other night, Bryce would have taken control of the situation, entered his woman, and passionately given her a real reason to moan. But Bryce didn't react. He couldn't. Instead, he sat silent, with Monica leaning back in-between his legs, unable to produce the necessary blood flow required to please his woman.

Nicole was pregnant.

So she said.

If it was true, what the hell was he going to do?

That's what Bryce was wondering while Monica stroked him, trying without success to get a rise out of him.

"Bryce, is something wrong?"

Bryce hadn't answered right away. Monica asked again. "Bryce . . . what's wrong?" Frustration had been laced in her tone.

"Nothing's wrong," he finally said.

"Then why are you not saying a word, and why the hell aren't you getting hard?"

Bryce sighed and ran his hand through his hair. As hard

as he tried, he just couldn't get Nicole off of his mind. He stood up and grabbed a towel. "I'm sorry baby," he said, stepping out of the tub, leaving Monica stunned. "I need to get going."

"Going? What do you mean you need to get going? Bryce, what the hell is wrong with you? And don't tell me 'nothing' again."

Bryce slipped into his boxers and avoided looking into her eyes. "I'm sorry, baby. For real. I jut have a lot of shit on my mind. Work-related things. I need to go home and do some thinking . . . come up with some ideas."

"What the–? You're kidding right?"

"I'm sorry, baby."

"Don't give me that 'baby' bullshit! This is supposed to be my goddamned night! Remember?"

"I know Monica. I promise I'll make it up to you."

"Make it up to me? Bryce . . . I swear you better not leave me like this."

"I'm sorry Monica. I really need to sort some things out."

"So what . . . you can't talk to me?"

"Not tonight."

"Not tonight? Goddamn it, Bryce. This shit can't be happening. You can't be doing this to me. Not tonight!"

"I'm sorry," Bryce said again.

As he walked out of the bathroom and went into the bedroom to get dressed, Monica screamed out, "Fuck you, Bryce!"

Slipping into a pair of jeans, Bryce clenched his jaws and cursed himself. He hated doing that to her, but he had no choice. He had to leave. Frustration and self-disappointment wouldn't allow for him to be there physically or mentally for his woman. He needed someone to talk to. But who?

It hadn't been a conscious decision to go to his brother's house, but twenty minutes later, that's where he ended up. He parked in his brother's driveway, got out of the car, walked up to the front door, and rang the bell.

"You forget how to use a phone?" Nate said, opening the door.

Bryce frowned. "I'm sorry, man . . . but I need to talk."

Nate looked at him and then opened the door wide. "Come on in."

"Damn, Bryce. Why the hell would you go and do something like that? Monica is a hell of a woman."

Sitting forward on his brother's couch, Bryce kept his eyes focused on a stain in his brother's carpeting. He didn't want to see the disappointment plastered on his brother's face. He'd been beating himself up enough as it was already. "I didn't plan for it to happen, man. It just did, and it got out of hand."

"I'd say so," Nate snapped. "Damn, man. Were you really that weak?"

"Don't come at me with your righteous shit, man. I really don't need to hear it right now. I'm not perfect like you are, alright?"

Nate clenched his jaws and shook his head. "Damn, Bryce. I mean you couldn't just hit it once and keep it moving? Your dick had to fall into her lap over and over again?"

"I told you man, I didn't mean to get caught up like that."

"So what . . . you just couldn't control yourself? What . . . did she have your ass under a spell?"

Bryce sighed. He wanted to say yes–that Nicole had indeed cast a spell over him with her extra-short mini-skirts, too-long and too-fine legs, tops she wore revealing more than enough cleavage, sexy side glances, and message-laden stares. Yes, Nicole had been a temptress. A witch who used her magical powers and wrapped her hands around him until he complied with her every wish, until he could no longer deny the fact that he wanted to palm her round ass, lift that skirt and go diving. That's what Bryce wanted to say.

Instead, a weak and mumbled, "She was attractive, Nate," is all that came out.

"I don't care how attractive she was," Nate said, louder than he intended. He quickly lowered his voice. He didn't want to wake Felicia or the kids. "Man . . . you fucked up! Royally. Don't you remember what that corny song said? Never trust a big butt and a smile. Poison, man. With her looks and her smile, Nicole poisoned you and now she's calling you her baby daddy."

Bryce slumped back into the couch. "I know."

Nate sat down beside him. "You know, huh? Man, what the fuck were you thinking? Monica is a bad ass woman. She's successful, she's independent, and she loves your ass to death."

"Yes . . . she is," Felicia said, stepping into the living room. Bryce and Nate turned around.

"Baby," Nate said quickly. "I didn't know you were up. I didn't mean to wake you."

Felicia yawned and joined the two brothers on the couch, taking her place beside her husband. But her eyes remained on Bryce, making him wonder how much of the conversation she'd heard. "You didn't wake me. I was up when you went to answer the door. Bryce . . . how could you?"

Bryce looked down to the carpet again.

"How could you go and be like every other man? I'm truly disappointed in you."

Bryce looked at his sister-in-law. Her lips were pressed firmly together to form a straight line, and darts flew from her eyes. As if his guilt and Nate's chastisement weren't bad enough, he now had to deal with Felicia. He kept his mouth closed. He wasn't in the mood to go head-to-head with a woman, especially over this topic. Unfortunately for him, Felicia didn't feel the same way.

"Men like you make me sick, Bryce. All that complaining you men do about not being able to find a good woman who appreciates, loves, and respects you is just a waste of breath. Because the minute you find the woman you've been wanting, what do you do? Go and screw around. Three years, Bryce. You've been with Monica for three years. You just had to have your cake and eat it too?"

Bryce looked to his brother hoping he would say something in his defense, but instead of speaking, Nate quietly rose from the couch and excused himself into the kitchen, leaving Bryce alone to burn under Felicia's heated gaze. *Thanks bro*, Bryce thought as he fixed his attention back on his sister-in-law.

"Look Felicia, I know what I did was wrong, but you beating me up is not what I need right now."

"Not what you need?" Felicia asked, stiffening her neck. Instantly, Bryce regretted his comment. "Just what the hell do you need, Bryce? Nicole's baby? Will that work for you? Excuse me for not feeling sorry for you, but you brought this all on yourself. Haven't you ever heard of protection? I mean, if you're going to be out there hoeing around, the least you could do is protect yourself. Is that how much you love Monica? Shit, you better be glad a baby is all you may end up with." Felicia pursed her lips, folded her arms across her chest, and gave him a scalding look. "I never expected this from you."

Bryce sighed and dragged his hands down over his face. Felicia was right and he had been so wrong. Just then, Nate came back into the living room with three glasses of juice. He gave Felicia hers, along with a kiss, and as he gave a glass to Bryce, he said, "She's right, man. You're lucky you didn't end up with an STD or worse."

"Yeah, I know, I know," Bryce mumbled. "Look guys, I didn't come here proud of what I did and expecting either one of you to be sympathetic towards me. I just need some advice. I don't know what the hell to do right now." Bryce lowered his head and watched the ice cubes in his glass, and mulled over how he felt just like one of the cubes, melting under Nate and Felicia's glares.

Felicia took a sip of her grape juice and took her brother-in-law's hand.

Bryce looked at her. He could tell by her eyes what she was wondering. "Nicole was the only one," he said.

Felicia nodded. "Do you love Monica?" she asked.

"Of course I do. You guys know that."

"Then if you love her, you're going to have to tell her."

Bryce pulled his hand away and stood up. "Tell her? Come on, if I do that, I'll lose her."

"Maybe . . . maybe not," Nate said. "She'll be mad and hurt yes, but just maybe, she'll be able to forgive you."

Bryce looked down at his brother. "There is no way in hell Monica would give me a second chance. She doesn't play that shit. The minute I tell her, our relationship will be finished."

"Well, Bryce," Felicia said softly. "As harsh as this may sound, you did the dirt. No one else. So this is your mess to clean up."

"But I don't want to lose her," Bryce said weakly.

"You have to tell her, man."

"But I don't even know if this baby is mine."

Felicia put her glass down on the coffee table, stood up, and put her hands on her hips. "Listen, Bryce . . . you can't keep this from Monica."

"Why not? At least until the baby comes and I can take a paternity test. Why should I tell her now? Especially if it turns out it's not mine."

"Little brother, look at what happened tonight, man. You're so stressed out over this shit that you couldn't

64

even chill and relax with your woman. If you're trippin' now, how the hell do you expect to hold shit together until the baby comes?"

"I don't know. Shit! I'll manage."

"Bryce . . . Monica has a right to know," Felicia said. "Trust me, from a woman's perspective it's better if she knew now. Because if it turns out this baby is yours and you don't tell her until after it's born, you'll be putting a nail in the coffin of your relationship for sure. There's no way Monica would forgive you for keeping this from her. Hell, I don't know many women who would. Tell her, Bryce. Tell her, and hope by some miracle that after she's calmed down, she may be willing to talk to you and possibly give you another chance."

"But . . ."

"No buts," Felicia said, cutting him off. "You brought this on yourself. Now if you say you love Monica, then you'll tell her. Tell her, and hope that she loves you enough to forgive you and somehow go forward. Whatever you do, don't wait until that baby comes." Without another word, Felicia turned, gave her husband a kiss, and headed toward the bedroom.

Bryce sat back down on the couch and without looking at his older brother, said, "I don't want to lose her, man."

Nate placed his hand on his brother's shoulder and stood up. "It really wouldn't be your choice, man. You know where the blankets and extra pillows are if you're staying. If not, make sure you lock the bottom lock on the door. I have to get up for work in the morning."

Nate headed toward the bedroom and his wife.

Back on the couch, Bryce finished his juice and exhaled. Tell Monica? How could he? He stood up and grabbed his car keys. As he drove home, he cursed Nicole, and more importantly, himself for ever playing with fire.

What the hell was he going to do?

8

Alex buttoned his shirt, slipped on his tie, and grabbed his laptop. He had to leave in fifteen minutes. He didn't like having to work the third shift in IT support. He wasn't comfortable leaving Karen alone at night. Although she could hold her own, Alex had been thinking about purchasing a dog. Nothing too fierce. Maybe a Doberman or a German shepherd. Something to make people think twice about walking through the door. Even though they lived in a relatively safe neighborhood, he never allowed himself to be so comfortable that he would let his guard down, because tragedy always happened when you became complacent and thought that all was right with the world. He knew better. And because the company was going through a strange transitional period, his night shift duties were going to be around for a while.

He knew Karen wasn't too fond of pets, so getting her to agree to the addition wasn't going to be easy. But Alex felt it was necessary. He would go to the pound tomorrow to look for one. If he could get some sleep, because he hadn't slept a wink all day. He'd tried, but it just didn't happen.

He had Mariah to thank for that.

It had been eight o'clock in the morning when she'd called. Alex had only been sleeping for two hours since coming in from work, and Karen had already gone to the television studio. With his eyes burning and demanding to be kept closed, Alex picked up the phone on the fourth ring. "Hello?"

"Alex, it's Mariah. There's a problem."

Immediately Alex's thoughts went to his son. His eyes popped open. "Is Miguel okay? What happened?"

Mariah huffed on the other end. "No!" she snapped.

"What's wrong with him?" Alex asked, his heart beating heavily.

"What's wrong with him? What's wrong with him? I'll tell you what's wrong with him."

Alex could tell by her tone that Miguel was okay and Mariah was about to try his patience again.

"What's wrong with my son is that wife of yours."

"Karen?"

"Yes, *Karen.* That damn bitch has Miguel comparing everything I do or say to her."

"Mariah, you're not making any sense."

"I can't do shit without Miguel saying 'Karen doesn't do it like that.' 'You don't cook like Karen.' 'Why don't you act like Karen?' 'Karen doesn't watch that.' On and on, I have to listen to that shit!"

Alex couldn't help but laugh.

"I don't find anything funny, Alex."

"Are you jealous, Mariah?"

"Fuck you, Alex. This has nothing to do with jealousy. This is about me being Miguel's mother and being respected. I don't know what the hell you two are putting into my son's head when he's with you, but I want that shit stopped."

"How can we stop something we're not doing, Mariah? We don't put anything into his head. Miguel is seven years old. He thinks for himself. Whatever he says or does is of his own accord."

"I know how old he is, asshole. I'm not a goddamned child."

"Then stop acting like one."

"*Vete para la mierda,* Alex."

"I'm in hell right now."

"*Maricon.*"

Alex exhaled. He'd had enough. "I'm getting off the phone now, Mariah."

"You better fix this problem, Alex. I am Miguel's mother. I don't want to be compared to that bitch in any way."

"Mariah, her name is Karen. Start using it. And as far as Miguel goes, did you ever stop to think that maybe he's saying those things because you're not doing something the right way?"

"Are you calling me a bad mother?"

Alex wanted to say yes, but held his tongue. He looked at the clock. He was losing valuable sleep time.

"Is that the kind of shit you're putting in my son's head?" Mariah continued. "That I'm a bad mother? I swear, Alex, if that's what you are doing, I will make our arrangement a legal one."

Alex clenched his jaw and squeezed his fingers around his temple. After Miguel's birth, he had somehow managed to convince Mariah that they didn't need to have a judge force him into being a responsible father. So instead of seeking child support, it was agreed between them that Mariah could have custody of Miguel, while Alex, who would have him on the weekends, gave Mariah twelve hundred dollars a month, five hundred of which was put into a savings account for Miguel that neither one of them could touch. The arrangement worked well for both of them.

"Look Mariah, not one month has gone by without me giving money. Money that you get to enjoy. So let's not go there."

Mariah banged on something in the background. "You know I could be getting a lot more money out of you, right? I swear you better set things straight before I do."

Just like a money-hungry bitch, Alex thought. "How many times are you going to threaten me with that shit, Mariah?"

"Oh, so you want me to make it a promise?"

Alex bit down on his bottom lip. He'd run out of patience. "You know what Mariah? You do whatever the fuck you feel you have to do to make you happy. But let me warn you, you better think long and hard before you do some stupid shit."

"Stupid?"

"Yeah, stupid. Because your ass has it good right now. You have custody of Miguel and you get to spend more than half of the fucking money I give. But I promise you, if you take this to the courts, you'll be sorry."

"What do you mean sorry?"

"Mariah, you work in the mall. You're not exactly pulling in the big bucks. The only reason you have Miguel is because I let you have him. But don't think for a second that I can't get full custody."

"Oh, so now you're the one making threats."

"No threat, Mariah. I'm just stating the facts. I'm the one living in a home that I own. I'm the one who makes triple what you make. I have every copy of every check I've ever made out for Miguel since his birth, which shows I don't need a court telling me to be responsible. If anyone has a right to have full custody, it's me."

"Whatever Alex. I'm his fucking mother."

"And I'm his father. Trust me when I say that you getting full custody won't be easy. The way you live your life with your here today, gone tomorrow boyfriends, you're not exactly going to win any special praise for being mother-of-the-year."

"Fuck you, Alex. As a matter of fact, fuck you and that bitch. You're not getting my son, and I will make your ass go broke with all the money you'll end up paying me!"

Mariah ended the call before Alex could say anything else. He never went back to sleep after that, and for the rest of the morning, he lay in bed and contemplated the thought of bringing Miguel to live with Karen and he full time.

He'd meant it when he told Mariah that Miguel was

with her because he allowed it. Whether he liked it or not, Mariah was the mother and the child's rightful place was with her. At least that's the way Alex was raised. Although he had both of his parents, he knew that if they had ever split up, Alex and his brothers would have lived with their mother full-time and seen their father on weekends. Thank God he never had to go through that. Miguel was holding up well, since splitting his time was all he knew. The thought of putting Miguel through the turmoil of a custody battle didn't sit well with him, but Mariah was forcing his hand. The uglier she became, the more he wanted his son away from her.

Alex slipped on his shoes and grabbed his keys. He would have to discuss the possibility with Karen. Although she loved Miguel, he wasn't sure what she would say, because having Miguel live with them would require her to take on motherly duties that she may not be ready for. Putting Miguel in his place on the weekends was one thing, but could she deal with it on a day-to-day basis? They'd talked about the possibility of starting their own family someday. Would Karen be ready?

9

Would Alex be ready to start a family? That was the big question. Karen rubbed her stomach, which was still relatively flat, save for a slight bulge, and sat down in her private office.

Pregnant.

She looked at the picture of her and Alex, along with Miguel, sitting on her desk. It was still almost hard to believe that there was going to be another addition soon. She rubbed her belly again. Hopefully, Alex would be all right with the news. It wasn't as though it wasn't going to happen eventually, Karen surmised, because they had been talking about starting a family of their own. That was something Karen wanted. Being a stepmother was fine, but she wanted her own child. At least with her, Alex didn't have to worry about the stress he got from Mariah.

Karen leaned back in her chair and stared at a few pictures of her with random local guests from her show. Ray

Lewis, Kwame Kilpatrick, Mayor Adrian Fenty. All great guests with great and real personalities. She was blessed.

She looked at the picture with her and Alex and Miguel again and wondered what Mariah's reaction was going to be. Not that she cared, but she still wondered. Would she have an ignorant and immature comment to make? Or, by some miracle, would she congratulate her? After all, besides Alex, the pregnancy would be the one thing they would have in common. Maybe they could finally be face-to-face without scowling and baring their claws, and have a pleasant conversation for once. Maybe Mariah could give her tips on how to deal with the weight gain or the vomiting, which Karen did like clockwork in the late afternoon.

Karen laughed out loud and said, "Fat chance."

She and Mariah had about as much of a chance being civilized with each other as Sarah Palin and a moose. The tension whenever they were in each other's presence was so thick at times, it could be cut with a dull butter-knife. And it's not that Karen hadn't tried with Mariah, because she really had. Even after their first encounter, Karen had made an attempt to get along with her. She'd say hi when she saw Mariah, and try to come up with something they could talk about, but nothing ever worked. Flat out, Mariah was an immature, jealous, inconsiderate, and indignant bitch. Too bad Alex had been a man and hadn't looked past her looks. Had he thought with his big head instead of his little one, neither he nor Karen would have to deal with Mariah and her pettiness.

Of course had the mistake never taken place, Miguel would have never been born, and Karen wouldn't have wanted that. Miguel was everything she would want in her own child. Intelligent, witty, inquisitive, charming, eager, and cute. Miguel was the kind of child Karen adored. Thankfully, he was looking and acting more and more like Alex each day. Sometimes it was hard to believe that as much of a devil as Mariah had been, she had been able to give birth to such an angel. That only added to the miracle of childbirth.

Karen's relationship with Miguel was a close one. In fact, at times, it could almost be comparable to a mother-son bond. Miguel may not have been her biological child, but she demanded respect nonetheless and she wasn't afraid to put him in his place. She loved him and she would be damned if she would allow him to grow to become another statistic. She was glad Alex didn't have a problem with her disciplining him. She liked the fact that her husband trusted her enough to deal with Miguel. It had been good practice for her. Having known him since he was three, Karen had gotten a lot of motherly experience and now she was ready for the real thing.

Karen rubbed her stomach again and smiled. She'd been doing that steadily since finding out that she was going to be a mother. She was excited about the new phase of her life. In a few months, she would be able to relate to the women who had children, who talked about them and their daily adventures. Having a baby was the ultimate task. Men may have bigger muscles, but women had all of the bragging rights. Until men could carry a child inside of them for nine months and spit them out through their little hole in the tip of their penis, men couldn't hold a candle to women. Karen was proud to know that she would soon be part of that special sisterhood. It was almost like being in a secret society. Until a woman gave birth, she was just like everyone else. Bearing a life into the world was like passing the ultimate test and achieving the special chair in the society.

Karen couldn't help but smile again. She was going to be a mommy. Alex . . . a daddy. She thought again about whether or not Alex would mind the addition. With all of the stress Mariah had been giving him over Miguel, she wasn't sure if he would agonize over the news or celebrate it. She was almost afraid to find out. But she would, when the timing was right. As she wondered when that time would be, her phone rang. Karen reached forward and answered it.

"Karen speaking."

"Hey, girl," Monica said on the other end.

"Hey, sis. How you doing?"

"I'm fine," Monica said, her voice solemn. "Just sitting here, relaxing."

Karen could hear the stress in her sister's voice.

"What's up girl? And don't say that you're fine, because I can tell you're not."

Five seconds of silence passed before Monica said, "I'm fine, Karen, really. OK? Anyway, how's the soon-to-be mommy feeling?"

"Unh uh. Don't even try that. I'm not buying that fine talk. Now tell your big sis what's wrong. Are you sick?"

"No, I'm not sick," Monica said.

"So what's wrong? Is work stressing you out?"

"Hardly. I just landed the biggest deal in the company's history yesterday."

"So you got the Redskins account?"

"I got it."

"Congrats! So what's the problem? As much as you've been talking about that damn account, I'd expect you to be bouncing off the walls right about now."

There was another brief moment of silence. Then Monica exhaled. "I am happy, girl. Believe me that account is going to do wonders for my career. If . . . no, when I help the Redskins' popularity and ticket sales increase, I'm sure I'll be looking at some lucrative offers. So much so that I may be able to actually leave the firm and do consulting on my own."

"I hear that, girl. So with everything pointing nowhere but up for you, why do you sound so down?"

"I'm just going through some issues."

"Issues? What kind of issues?"

"Relationship issues."

"Oh, I see. What's going on with you and Bryce?"

"Nothing that I can't handle, sis."

"Come on, Monica. I know you called to vent. I can tell. So speak."

Monica exhaled. "Karen, last night Bryce came over to my place. It should have been an incredible night. I was feeling good and I wanted to *celebrate*. I mean, hell, with all of the work I'd been doing lately, sex is the one thing that I haven't been getting enough of."

"I hear that, girl. So what happened?"

"Karen, I don't even know. Instead of getting our freak on, I ended up spending the night alone."

"Alone?"

"Yes, alone. Fucking alone."

"Why? What went wrong?"

"Girl, I wish I knew. The mood was so right. We had champagne, candles, bubble bath–Teddy crooning from the stereo."

"You had Teddy? Which one? 'Come and Go with Me' or 'Turn Out the Lights'?"

"'Come and go with me.'"

"That is my song, girl. That song'll make you have babies. Anyway, what was the problem?"

"I'm still trying to figure that out. I mean, one minute we're in the tub and the next he gets up and leaves."

"What? Why?"

"I have no clue. He tried to make up some excuse about having shit to do or think about for work, but I wasn't even trying to buy that."

"Why not?"

"Girl, when we were in the tub, I was stroking him, trying to get him worked up for some lovin'."

"And what happened?"

"Karen . . . Bryce didn't even get hard."

"What do you mean he didn't get hard?"

"I mean his shit was softer than wet cotton."

"Damn."

"Exactly. Now I don't know about you, but I don't know any man that has ever let work get in the way of some ass."

"So what are you saying? That he was lying about work being on his mind?"

"I don't know. All I'm saying is that as long as I've been with Bryce, I've never known him to have a problem getting an erection."

"Maybe it's medical. Maybe he needs some Viagra. He is thirty," Karen joked.

Monica laughed. "Please. The last thing my man needs is some damn Viagra. His tool works, and works very well."

"Not last night it didn't," Karen said bluntly.

Monica sighed. "No . . . it didn't."

"So what do you think could be the reason for the lack of attention, all puns intended?"

"Yeah, whatever. I've been thinking about it all day, but I just can't come up with a reason."

Karen looked at a picture sitting on the corner of her desk, of her and her sister. It was taken at Virginia Beach on the boardwalk. They had gone there on an all girls getaway two summers ago. "Sis, let me say something, and I don't want you to take this the wrong way, okay?"

"Sure."

"Listen, I know you love Bryce and I know that you trust him, but I'm gonna be honest with you. Since you've stated that a medical condition is not plausible, then I have to say that the only other time a man has a problem getting an erection, especially when he's being stroked, is if there's another woman in the picture. About the only other excuse would be if he's not attracted to his partner, and I know Bryce is attracted to you. So . . ." Karen didn't say another word. She figured she had said enough.

She liked Bryce and thought he'd been good for Monica, but he was still a man. And as her father had shown, it didn't matter what a man may or may not have done for a woman, being a man was almost enough to get him implicated. So far she hadn't had to deal with that with Alex, but don't think her eyes were closed to the possibilities. She knew that he liked to look, which she was okay with, because she enjoyed the use of her eyes too. But looking was all Alex had better be doing.

"I hear what you're saying, but Bryce is *not* fooling around on me. He is nothing like the minister."

"I'm not saying he is, Monica. All I'm saying is that the possibility is there, and it may be something you may want to keep your eyes opened to."

Monica breathed out heavily. Karen could tell her sister was annoyed, but she didn't care.

"Well thank you for your professional advice, but like I said, I'm not worried about Bryce, nor do I need to worry about him. He respects me, just as I respect him. But tell me, sister dear, do you follow your own advice, or do you believe in the sanctity of your marriage?"

Karen rolled her eyes. "I believe in my marriage little sister, and I definitely practice what I preach. I'm no fool, nor will I ever allow myself to be played for one." A tense moment of silence took place after Karen's response.

Karen was waiting for and fully expected another snap from Monica. But it never came. "Look," she said softly. "I'm sorry for snapping. I'm just a little frustrated right now. I haven't even spoken to Bryce since last night."

"Why not?"

"I guess he's waiting for me to call. But I'm not going to. Shit, he left. I didn't."

"Good move."

"But anyway, I didn't really call to bitch and complain. The reason I called was to ask if you'd spoken to Mama lately?"

"She called you too?" Karen asked.

"Yeah."

"She mention the dinner?"

"Yeah."

"She invited Alex. Weird huh?"

"Very," Monica said. "I wonder if she called Jeff?"

"I don't know."

"How long has it been since you last spoke to him?"

"It's been a while."

"Same here," Monica said. "I tried to reach him a couple of times, but he never called me back. And I'd been so busy nabbing that Redskins account, I never got a chance to try again."

"He's probably too busy running around with some female anyway," Karen said. "You know how he is."

"Yes I do. He's just like the minister. So much so that it makes it hard for me to be close to him. I really hope for his and his future wife's sake, that he changes."

"Don't forget any future kids too," Karen said.

"Oh, especially for the kids' sake. Anyway, enough about our baby brother, what do you make of Mama's birthday decision?"

Karen shrugged. "Well, it's her birthday, so if she wants to cook, she has that right."

"Yeah, I guess. I just can't shake the feeling that this is more than a dinner. There was something in her voice. . . .

I can't put my finger on it, but it was almost as if something was heavy on her mind."

"Yeah, I know what you mean. When she called, she actually asked me how Alex was. I was shocked. But when she said she wanted him to come to the dinner, it did make me wonder."

"Mama has never been one of Alex's biggest fans."

"No, she certainly hasn't."

"I hope she's okay. Maybe we should call her on the three-way and talk to her. Maybe together we can get her to open up to us."

Karen thought for a minute. "No, let's not. I'm sure she's all right. Besides, even if she wasn't she wouldn't say. You know how stubborn Mama can be when she's ready."

Monica agreed. "True. I guess we'll just have to wait for the dinner before we make any assumptions."

"It's better that we do. To be honest, I'd kind of just like to enjoy the fact that she mentioned Alex in a positive light."

Monica chuckled. "I figured you had a better chance of winning the lottery before that would happen."

"I know what you mean, girl."

"Did you tell Alex about the invitation yet?"

"No. I will when I speak to him though. He's going to be shocked."

"I'm sure he will be," Monica agreed.

Karen's palm pilot suddenly beeped. "Hey, girl, I have to get going. I have a meeting in a few."

"Okay, handle your business. The show is still great by the way. I tape it so I can watch it when I get home."

"That's good to know. I really appreciate your support."

"Hey, I'm your sister. I'm obligated to watch it."

"Gee thanks."

"You know I'm kidding. Just don't forget about me, when you go national and blow up like Oprah."

"Impossible, girl. Besides, I'll need some extra help on my staff."

"Gee thanks," Monica said with a laugh. "I love you, Karen."

"Love you too, sis," Karen said with a smile.

"Hey, did you tell Alex about the baby yet?"

Karen's smile broadened. "Not yet, but I will."

"OK. Let me know how that goes."

"You'll be the first to know. Good luck with Bryce, and keep me posted. Maybe I can do a show about you two. Men who can't get it up and then get out."

"That's foul," Monica said unable to contain her laughter.

"Hey, if Jerry can do it—"

"Good-bye, Karen," Monica cut in.

Karen laughed with her sister. "Talk to you later. And for real, don't stress over it. I'm sure things will be okay."

"We'll see. Bye."

"Bye." Karen hung up the phone and grabbed her organizer and stood up. Before walking away from her desk, she took a look at the picture of her and Monica again. It was the only family picture she had in her office. "Don't be blind, girl," she whispered. Then she looked at the one of her and Alex again. She loved him with all her heart and couldn't imagine what she'd do if he ever betrayed their trust, although she did have some Lorena Bobbitt in her.

She shook her head. She didn't want her thoughts to go there. She left for her meeting and filled her head with thoughts and images of Alex's expression when she would tell him the news of the addition to their family.

10

It was Friday night and Karen was home. Alone.

She wasn't used to either one of those predicaments, because before Alex's shift change and she became pregnant, she was either getting her Friday groove on, or she was home snuggling with Alex and getting their own private groove on. But this wasn't before. Alex had to work nights for God knew how long, and with a baby in her oven, Karen couldn't party like she used to.

She flipped through the channels on the television aimlessly. She still hadn't had a real chance to tell him yet. His working the third shift was really getting in the way. When she was home, he wasn't, vice versa. She could have called and told him, or awakened him to tell him, but she wanted him standing in front of her and she wanted him alert. But she couldn't and wouldn't wait much longer. Her third month was coming.

She was tired and fighting sleep, but she didn't want to miss Alex's goodnight call—something he did every night. Until she started experiencing it herself, she had no idea what her body would be going through. The constant vomiting, the complete exhaustion, the constant need to urinate, the hormonal upheaval—being pregnant was no picnic. And she was only in the first trimester. She still had the weight gain, the back pain, the possible constipation and please-no-diarrhea to look forward to. But she couldn't wait. She also couldn't wait to tell Alex the news. She wanted to do it before he left for work, but she had to stay late to deal with some issues for the show and hadn't been able to leave early like she wanted to. By the time she finally made it home, Alex had gone.

She thought of telling him when he called, but again, she wanted to see his reaction when she did.

A baby.

She couldn't wait to see Alex in the morning. She decided she would tell him first thing so they could celebrate for a few hours before he went to pick up Miguel. She wondered what Miguel would say when he found out he was going to have a half-sibling. She thought of his smile, the carbon copy of Alex's, and wondered whose smile her baby would have. Or whose eyes and whose nose. Karen smiled at the thought. Then her phone rang. She looked at the time. It was still early—nine o'clock. She checked the caller ID; it was Alex. He usually called around eleven to tuck her in. She picked up the phone anxious to hear his voice and doubtful that she would be able to keep the secret until the morning. "Hey baby," she said in a singsong voice. "I didn't expect to hear from you yet."

"Hey sexy," Alex answered. "I know I usually call later, but we're having a major crisis right now. Some genius over in project management decided to tell their vendor to go ahead and cancel some circuits earlier today. Of course they never needed to be cancelled in the first place, so now we have red alarms going off like crazy and AOL is pissed because thousands of customers have lost their access to the Net."

Karen could hear the frustration in his voice. The news would definitely wait for the morning. "That sounds terrible, baby. I mean, I have no idea what you're talking about, but it sounds bad."

"Bad is not the word. Anyway, I didn't think I'd get the chance to call later so I wanted to call and tuck you in now, even though you're not going to bed yet."

"Actually, I'm in bed right now."

"Already?"

"Yeah, I'm beat. I can barely keep my eyes open. I have the TV on trying to stay awake because I didn't want to miss your call."

"You know, you've been sleeping a lot lately. Heavier too. Maybe you should take a couple of days off. I know the show is your life and you're trying to go to the next level, but some days off might be good for you."

Karen smiled. "I'll be taking some time off soon enough."

"What does that mean?"

"Nothing baby. Just that I'll follow your advice soon."

"OK. Well listen, I have to get going. I love you. I miss you. And I'll see you in the morning."

"Okay, baby. I miss and love you too. Good luck with the crisis."

"Thanks. Good night and have sweet dreams."

Karen hung up the phone. She missed her man being next to her at night. Steamy dreams weren't nearly good enough. She couldn't wait until he went back to his regular hours. The third shift was putting a damper on their sex life, which wasn't what she wanted, because from what her friends who'd gone through the joys and pains of pregnancy said, sex would be the last thing she would want.

She turned off the television and finally allowed her eyes to close. The fatigue was one of the worst things about being pregnant, because no matter how much sleep she got, she constantly felt as though she'd run the New York Marathon. Within seconds she started to drift off, and then the phone rang again. She didn't want to answer it at first, but she figured Alex had forgotten something. She answered without checking the ID. "Couldn't get enough of my voice, huh sexy?"

"Oh please," Mariah said on the other end.

Karen's eyes snapped open immediately. "Mariah?"

"It sure as hell isn't who you thought it was," Mariah snapped.

Karen rolled her eyes and breathed out hard. "What do you want, Mariah?"

"Where's Alex?"

"He's at work. You should know that."

"Well . . . I need to speak to him."

"Like I said, he's at work. What did you need?"

"I said I need to speak with *him*. Not you."

"Look Mariah, I'm not in the mood. If you want to talk to Alex so bad, then call him there. You have the number. But let me just tell you that he's busy, so he may not have much time for you."

"Whatever."

Karen exhaled. She was tired of putting up with Mariah's shit. "Mariah, your nasty attitude is tired already. Why don't you grow the hell up?"

"Why don't you disappear . . . permanently?"

Karen squeezed her eyes closed as her temperature rose. She breathed out slowly in an attempt to calm down. The last thing she needed was to get into an argument. "Mariah, I'm not going to stoop down to your level, okay? So just go and call Alex, and let's end this before it gets out of hand." She was about to hang up the phone, but before she could, Mariah spoke out.

"Tell him he can't pick up Miguel this weekend because I'm going out of town and I'm taking him with me."

"Mariah, you know you can't do that. Alex gets Miguel every weekend. You can't just change things at the last minute. Besides, he's already made plans to take Miguel somewhere tomorrow."

"Look *pendeja*, Miguel is my son and not yours, and I can damn well take him when I want, where I want. I answer to nobody. *Especially* not you."

"Mariah, why don't you act like a mother then?"

"Excuse me?"

"You heard me. Why don't you start paying attention to your son instead of being a vindictive, jealous, ignorant bitch with me?"

"Jealous? Of your ass? Please. And don't you even try to say I don't take care of my child."

"Come off of it, Mariah. Everyone knows that Omar and Ellen take more care of your son than you do."

"Who the hell are you to talk about being a mother? Get a child first, and then come at me with that shit."

"You know what Mariah, I'll know all about being a mother soon, because I'm pregnant."

"Pregnant?"

"Did I stutter?"

"Fuck you, *puta!*"

"No, fuck you, Mariah. Maybe after my baby is born, you can come by and I can give *you* lessons on motherhood."

"I'll show you what a fucking lesson is, bitch."

"Whatever, Mariah. I'm not scared of your despicable ass."

"I don't care if you're pregnant, bitch. I will kick your ass."

"Mariah, if you come anywhere near me, pregnant or not, I will beat your ass twice. Once for me, and another time for my child."

"Fuck you, *negra!*"

"Is cursing and acting ignorant all you can do, Mariah?"

Mariah rambled off in Spanish for a few seconds before saying, "Dumb-ass bitch!" and then the line went dead.

Karen put the phone down and inhaled deeply. She hadn't meant to tell Mariah about the pregnancy, but she couldn't avoid it. Mariah had worked her first, second, and last nerve. "Bitch," she whispered. She picked up the phone and dialed Alex's number. When he answered, she didn't hesitate to hold her tongue.

"You better get Mariah's ass in check, Alex."

Alex groaned. "What did she do now?"

Karen sucked her teeth. "Tell that bitch she better quit with her petty threats, because I am not the one."

"Calm down, baby. Just tell me what happened."

"She called here a few minutes ago looking for you. I swear, Alex, tell her to stay away from me."

"Karen, will you please calm down. I'll handle her. I promise. Now did she say what she wanted?"

"Yes she did, and you're not going to like it one bit."

"What else is new?" Alex asked. "What did she say?"

"She said you can't take Miguel this weekend because she's going away."

"So? She's gone away before."

"Well, she said she's taking Miguel with her."

"No the hell she's not. I get Miguel on the weekends. She can't go changing plans at the last second."

"I told her that. But you know how she is."

"Goddammit!" Alex said slamming his hand down on the desk. "Baby, I have to take care of some things here. I'll call Mariah and deal with her."

"Please do. I'm not trying to get arrested for kicking her behind."

"Don't worry, baby. I'll talk to her. I have to go. Sleep tight."

"Oh, I'm tight alright," Karen, said. She hung up the phone. She was too angry to fall back asleep. Ignorant bitch, she thought. As Karen channel surfed over the next hour, she wondered if tomorrow would be a good time to tell Alex about the baby. She knew that once he finished dealing with Mariah, he wouldn't be in the best of moods. Karen pressed angrily on the remote, pretending that each button was Mariah's head.

11

Alex walked in his home and slammed the door harder than he'd meant to. He'd been slamming a lot of things. He dropped his keys on the side table in the hallway, and walked into the living room. He was too angry to go to bed and he didn't want to wake Karen. He picked up a picture of Miguel and stared at it. Mariah's last minute decision to take Miguel with her on a weekend getaway had Alex ticked. His mind flashed back to the conversation he'd had with her after speaking with Karen.

"What do you mean I can't pick up Miguel tomorrow?" He hadn't even waited for her to say hello.

"Sergio is taking me to Busch Gardens tomorrow and I'm taking Miguel. It was a last minute decision."

"Mariah, since when do you take Miguel anywhere? And who the fuck is Sergio?"

"Sergio is a friend. And I do take Miguel places."

Alex sat down at his desk and squeezed the hell out of his stress ball. "A friend? I've never heard you mention him before."

"*Eres mi padre?*" Mariah asked.

"It's not about me being your father, Mariah. First of all, you know I get Miguel on the weekends. I don't care what last minute decision you make. We have an arrangement. You just can't go changing shit. But more importantly, I don't care what you do or who you do it with; I don't want my son going anywhere with some stranger."

"Miguel is my son too, Alex. And don't you even try to go there with me, because you certainly didn't tell me shit about Karen."

Alex thought to himself for a moment. He'd been with Karen for five months before he brought Miguel around her. He didn't know what type of person Sergio was, but he knew what Karen was about and what her motives were. He trusted her to be around his son, and the fact that he loved her didn't hurt either. Alex was sure Mariah didn't know shit about Sergio, and she sure as hell didn't know anything about love.

"How long have you known this guy Mariah? Because if I remember correctly, last month you were talking to Javier."

"What does it matter, Alex? I trust Sergio enough to put my life in his hands."

"Mariah, I don't really give a fuck who you trust your life with. I care about Miguel. I don't want him around some guy you've only known for a month, if that."

"Well too fucking bad, Alex. Miguel is my son and he lives with me. He comes with me."

"He's my son too, dammit. I have a right to take him."

"You want to pay more money for those rights, Alex?"

"You're a fucking bitch, Mariah."

"And you're an asshole. And you better get your wife in check before I—"

"Before you what?" Alex yelled cutting her off. "You better not go anywhere near her, Mariah."

"Or what Alex? What the fuck, are you going to do? Hit me? Please do. I would love to tell the judge about your woman-beating ways."

"Mariah, don't test me."

"Whatever, Alex. You can see Miguel next weekend."

When Mariah hung up the phone, Alex slammed the receiver down and in a fury, swept papers, pens, and whatever else lay scattered on his desk, to the floor. He pounded his fist on his desktop so hard that some of his coworkers rushed into his office thinking something had been wrong. After apologizing, Alex took a long break and called and woke up his parents for advice. That conversation lasted fifteen minutes with his father saying simply: "Miguel es tu hijo."

Alex hung up the phone, knowing that he would have to tell Karen he wanted custody of Miguel. That's what he was thinking about when Karen appeared in the living room behind him. He'd heard her slippers shuffling on the hardwood floor before she said, "Hey, baby."

He turned and stared at his wife. Her eyes were puffy from sleeping and her hair disheveled, yet all he could think was that no woman had been more beautiful. She walked up to him and kissed him softly on the lips.

"Did I wake you?" Alex asked.

"Yup."

Alex frowned. "Didn't mean to be so loud. Sorry."

"Believe me, baby, I understand."

"I'm glad you do, because there's something I want to talk about."

"Okay, baby. I have something to talk about too."

Alex looked at her curiously. "Ladies first."

"No, you go ahead." Karen moved from him and sat down on their beige leather sofa. Alex looked at the picture of Miguel again and then looked at one with him, Karen and Miguel.

"I'm going to fight for full custody of Miguel. I can't take this shit with Mariah anymore. I'd rather take my chance in court than be at her mercy all because I don't want to pay an arm and a leg in child support, which I really may not have to do because I am in a better position than she is. Now I know we're married, which means we have a partnership, but I've been doing a lot of thinking about this, and last night just really helped to make up my mind.

"Want to tell me what happened?"

Alex shook his head. "No. I don't feel like reliving the drama."

Karen shook her head and then counted to five in her head. Before she reached four, Alex opened his mouth.

"She went to Busch Gardens with some guy she's known no longer than a fucking month! She even had the nerve to say that because she trusted her life in his

96

hands, Miguel would be okay too. Baby, I could have strangled her when she said that. She's lucky she wasn't standing in front of me. For all she knows, this character could be a rapist or worse, a pedophile. Personally I don't give a shit what happens to her, but that's my son. I don't want to take the chance that something could happen to him just because she wants to be an irresponsible trick. I want Miguel, and I will do whatever I have to do to get him.

"I know we've talked about having a family of our own and I'm not trying to force motherhood on you, but I need my son. I need to know that he'll be okay. I won't be able to be at peace as long as Mariah has him."

Alex paused and stared at Karen, who'd remained silent during his explanation. He tried to read his wife, to get an idea of what she'd been thinking as she stared down at the floor. "Baby, I didn't make this decision to upset you. I know I should have discussed this with you, but getting Miguel is just something that I have to do. If something ever happened to him, I don't know what I'd do. I love my son, and I can't shake the feeling that as long as he is with her, something bad will happen. I hope you understand what I'm saying."

He watched Karen intently. The last thing he wanted was to be at odds with her, but whether she was happy or not, Alex had made up his mind.

"I'm pregnant, Alex," Karen finally said softly.

Alex's head snapped back. "What . . . did you say?"

Karen lifted her head. "I'm pregnant. We're having a baby."

Alex massaged the back of his neck. "Are you serious?"

Karen nodded yes. Alex smiled and moved toward her, lifted her from the sofa, threw his arms around her, and kissed her on the forehead. Instinctively, Karen's arms wrapped around his small waistline. When Alex finally let her go, he noticed that she'd been crying. He kissed her again. "What's wrong, baby?"

Karen sniffed and wiped her eyes with the back of her hand. "You're . . . you're okay with the news?"

"Am I okay? Am I okay? Of course I am. How could I not be?"

"After everything you just said, I was afraid that the last thing you would want would be another child."

Alex shook his head. "Baby, I love you. A baby! How many months are you?"

"Three."

"A baby!" Alex dropped to his knee, lifted her t-shirt and kissed her belly. "A baby. Our baby." He stood up and cradled her face in both of his hands. "Are you okay with me wanting Miguel?"

Karen smiled as tears snaked from her eyes. "Of course I am. Honestly, it's about time you go after custody."

"And you don't feel like I'm forcing motherhood on you?"

Karen smirked. "Hello. I'm pregnant. Motherhood is here, Miguel or no Miguel. So no, I don't feel as though you're forcing it on me. Besides, I love that little boy."

Alex kissed his wife again and stared into her eyes. "What did I do to get so lucky?"

Karen smiled devilishly. "You are lucky, aren't you," she said, kissing his chin. Alex marveled again about the beauty that she possessed both inside and out. Kissing her softly on her lips, Alex took Karen by the hand and led her back to the bedroom to celebrate.

12

In the three years Bryce and Monica had been together, the longest they'd ever gone without speaking had been two days. The reason that happened had been because Monica had been away on a business trip and she hadn't been able to get ahold of Bryce because his cell phone had been stolen and the phone lines in his neighborhood had been down. At least those are the excuses Bryce had given Monica. The truth was, he had been with Nicole, taking advantage of the time away from Monica, not realizing that he would pay for it later by sitting at home stressing over the possibility of becoming a father.

From the very beginning, Bryce and Monica promised each other that as long as they could prevent it, they would never let a day go by without speaking. They were a team and they both knew that a team's success was dependent upon the open lines of communication. So they talked about little things, big things, and everything in between. Only once had Bryce ever allowed Nicole to come between that promise.

Now it was happening again.

Bryce exhaled as he sat in the living room of his two-bedroom condominium, listening to Alicia Keys's song, "A Woman's Worth." The truth of his dilemma was being sung in her chorus: *A real man knows a real woman.*

Bryce took a long swallow of the beer that he held in his hand. He inhaled and exhaled again. Five days had now gone by since he'd left Monica sitting stunned in her bathtub. Not one time had she tried to call him, which hadn't surprised him because she never made the first move, especially if she wasn't the one at fault. Bryce hadn't tried to call her either, nor had he gone by her place to apologize or explain. He just couldn't. He wasn't ready to face her. He didn't want to look in her chocolate brown eyes and tell her the truth; that while she was busy being a real woman, he had been doing his best to be anything but a real man. Had he been a man, he would never have taken Monica's worth for granted.

Pregnant.

The word whispered through his mind again somewhere during the middle of Alicia Keys's piano rift. He'd seen Nicole earlier in the week. He'd called her and met her for lunch. He wanted to see the signs, to see if she'd been telling the truth. The slight belly protruding through her shirt and the obvious weight gain had been proof enough. The meeting had been short and unpleasant.

"You believe me now, Bryce?" Nicole had asked, as he stared at her silently.

They were tucked away in the back against the far wall

of Don Pablo's. Nicole wanted to eat there because she had a craving for enchiladas. Bryce kept his back to the other diners. He'd tried to convince her to meet somewhere else because Don Pablo's was one of Monica's favorite lunch spots, but Nicole wasn't having it.

"How do you know this baby is mine, Nicole?" Bryce asked, trying to keep his voice low.

"You calling me a ho, Bryce?"

"Look Nicole, I know I wasn't the only brother you were sleeping with." Actually he didn't, but that was what he had hoped.

"Fuck you, Bryce!" Nicole snapped loud enough to cause an older woman in the table beside them to humph.

"I already did and look where it got me," Bryce answered back.

Nicole curled her lips to reply, and out of nowhere her lips began to quiver and her eyes welled with tears. "Don't you even care? I'm pregnant with your baby. Doesn't that mean anything to you?"

Bryce passed his hand through his hair and tried to ignore the stares coming from the people around him. Great, he thought. He'd picked the back for privacy, and Nicole's tears weren't helping. He grabbed a napkin and tried to hand it to her, but instead of taking it, she slapped his hand away.

"You're an ass, Bryce. You're a typical poor excuse for a Black man and just like the rest of them, you're afraid to handle your responsibility." Nicole pushed herself away from the table. "You know something," she said slinging her purse over her shoulder, "the only reason I never told my father about us after you used me the way you did was because at the time I loved you. Yes, I know you were with Monica and we were supposed to just be fuck buddies, but I was stupid. Stupid enough to think and hope by some miracle that you would see I was better for you. But you know what? I'm not stupid, I don't love you, and I will be telling my father that I'm carrying your baby. He'll be pissed, but at least I won't have to worry about losing my job!" Nicole spat in Bryce's face and stormed off, leaving him alone, embarrassed, and wondering if she would indeed tell his boss.

Bryce took another swallow of beer as his phone rang. He looked at the caller ID. It was Alex's cell phone. He answered on the third ring. "What's up, man?" he said trying to sound happier than he was.

"What's going on future brother-in-law? Why you sounding all solemn?"

Bryce shook his head. He thought he'd masked his frustration well.

"My bad, Alex. I'm just here chilling. What's going on with you? Why do you sound like you won the lottery?"

"Because I did!" Alex exclaimed.

"What?"

"Come on man. I'm surprised you didn't call to congratulate me."

"Congratulate you? You really won the lottery? Because if you did, I'm cashing in on the fifty you owe me from the basketball game, plus an extra million in interest."

"I paid that back to you in drinks."

"Alright, well I want half."

"Half? For what?"

"For not telling Karen about how you love to twirl women around on the dance floor."

Alex laughed. "That's cold, man."

Bryce laughed for the first time all day.

"Anyway," Alex continued. "I didn't win the lottery, so you can just keep your mouth zipped."

"So what do I need to congratulate you for?"

"You really don't know?"

"Wouldn't ask if I did," Bryce said.

"I'm gonna be a dad, again. Karen's pregnant!"

At the mention of the word, Bryce's mood instantly changed. "Really?" he asked.

"Yeah, man. She's almost three months. Damn, I'm surprised Monica didn't break the news to you."

"It must have slipped her mind," Bryce said.

"Maybe. So, can a Puerto Rican brother get a congratulations or what?"

"My bad, man . . . congratulations," he said, hoping he hadn't sounded too unenthused.

"Anyway, I'm calling because I want to celebrate. I figured the four of us could go to dinner. Matter of fact, let's make it six. Call Nate and Felicia, and tell them to come too."

Bryce sighed. Any other time he'd have hopped off the phone, called Monica and then Nate, but he couldn't do that now. "Man, I'd love to do that, but I don't think that's a good idea right now."

"Man, what is up with you?"

"Nothing man. It's just . . ." He paused. He wanted to open up to Alex, but didn't want to put his business out there. But then he figured Monica had probably already done that with Karen. "Man, Monica and I aren't speaking right now."

"Now it's my turn to say, 'really?' " Alex said. "What's up with you two lovebirds?"

Bryce closed his eyes and slumped further down in the sofa. "Alex, I fucked up."

"Fucked up? What do you mean fucked up?"

"Man, I was messing with this woman from work a while back and last week she called me and told me that she's four months pregnant. She says it's mine."

"Are you serious, dude? You're not bullshitting me?"

Bryce sighed. "I wish I was, man. Believe me, I really do. But that's not all."

"There's more?"

"Yeah. The woman is my boss's daughter. I met her for lunch today, and she's talking about telling her father."

"Damn," Alex whispered. "Why the hell would you fuck with your boss', daughter?"

"Man, in the beginning, I didn't know. She uses her mother's maiden name so that no one knows they're father and daughter. By the time I found out, it was too late to stop."

"Damn," Alex said again. "How did Monica find out?"

"She didn't . . . yet."

"She didn't? I'd just assumed that since you two haven't spoken, it was because she found out."

"No, she hasn't yet. But I may have to tell her. I'm confused right now. On one hand, I need to tell her. This isn't exactly something I can keep a secret, you know.

But on the other hand, I don't want to tell her because I don't know for sure if this baby is mine, and I don't want to say anything if I don't have to."

"I don't know what to say, man."

"You don't have to say anything," Bryce said. "Because I've already said and thought everything. So have Nate and Felicia."

"You told them?"

"Yeah. I went to get advice from Nate, and Felicia overheard."

"Damn. I know that wasn't pretty."

"Not at all. She didn't hesitate to lay into me, which only made me feel worse than I already did."

"Do you really feel bad?" Alex asked. "Or do you feel bad because the woman is pregnant?"

"Alex, when I first started messing around with her, I'll be honest; I didn't really feel anything. I was just being a man and busting my nut on the side. But once I realized how much I loved Monica, I regretted ever having slipped up. I ended things with Nicole because I wanted Monica to be my every, and only thing, just like I was to her. I love her, man, and this shit is eating me up inside. That's why we haven't spoken. The last time we were together, we were naked in her tub and were supposed to be celebrating her landing a huge account."

"Yeah, I heard she got the Redskins deal. So what happened with the celebration?"

"Nothing happened. I was so stressed over this shit, I couldn't even perform."

"Damn, Bryce. That's serious."

"Tell me about it. That shit has never happened to me before."

"What do Nate and Felicia think you should do?"

"They both say I should tell Monica and let the chips fall where they may. But like I said, what if this kid isn't mine? Do I really want to blow up my spot like that?"

"But what if it is yours?" Alex countered. "If you don't tell her and the baby is yours, then you will definitely lose her. If you tell her now, you may have a better chance at being forgiven."

"What if she never wants to see me again?"

"Hey, that's possible. Look, I know all about mistakes and their consequences. I deal with Mariah, remember?"

"Yeah, but you never had another woman to lose."

"No I didn't. But I have Mariah, and she's worse than three women combined."

"Alright. I'm gonna tell, Monica, man," Bryce decided after a brief moment of silence. "I was a coward by stepping out on her. The least I can do is be a man now."

"That's the right decision, man. Tough, but the right one to make."

"I swear I don't want to lose her."

"I know you don't. But the hard reality is that you may. That'll be Monica's decision to make though. Either way, man, I'm here for you. You're my friend and hopefully, you'll be my brother-in-law someday. I got your back."

"Thanks Alex. That means a lot."

"Hey, Karen just came in. I'm gonna jet before she gets up in our conversation. Good luck, man."

"Thanks. I'll need it."

Bryce hung up the phone and downed the rest of his beer, which had gone warm. As he slipped on his sneakers and grabbed his keys, he wondered if Monica would realize his worth. He left to find out.

13

Monica sat alone in her living room and cried. She'd been doing that steadily for the past two days. She'd gone through a gamut of emotions since Bryce had walked out on her. At first she felt shock. She couldn't believe he had up and left the way he did. On day two she experienced anger. Who the hell was he to leave with a tired excuse and not call to apologize, explain, or make things up to her? Day three had been the same as day two. By day four, the anger had been replaced by self-blame. What had she done to cause him to leave and not call her? Tears fell that day. Day five was like day four, only the torrent fell harder. Did Bryce still love her?

That's what she wondered as she sat in darkness and silence. She wanted to call him, but her pride wouldn't allow it. Like she'd told Karen, Bryce left. She hadn't. But why did he leave? Why had he been so distant in the tub when they should have been so close? Could Karen be right? Could Bryce have been fooling around? Is that why he hadn't called? Because he'd been out with some other woman?

Tears fell harder down her cheeks. She didn't want to believe that Bryce could be like the men she'd heard her girlfriends complain about, but for the first time, she had doubts about her man. She looked at her phone sitting on her end table and willed it to ring. Please call me, she thought to herself. But instead of a ringing telephone, the doorbell chimed. Monica hurried to wipe her tears away. She wasn't expecting company and she knew not to hope that it would be Bryce. But she did. And when she checked through the peephole and saw him standing outside, she didn't move. It was almost hard to believe that he was actually there, as if it weren't him, but a mere figment of her imagination conjured up by her desire. She pinched herself. She wasn't dreaming. She wiped her eyes again, but knew that was of no use because her puffy eyes would be a dead giveaway.

She opened the door.

Neither one of them spoke. They just stared at each other.

"Hey," Bryce finally said.

Monica didn't respond.

"Mind if I come in?" Bryce asked.

Monica turned and walked away, leaving the door open. Bryce's shoulders slumped. He stepped inside, closed the door, and walked to the living room where Monica had turned on the light and was sitting on the sofa.

Bryce sat down in the loveseat facing her. "How have you been?"

"Fine. Just fine," Monica said laced with sarcasm. After all of the crying, her anger was beginning to resurface.

"How's work?"

Monica stared at him in disbelief. "You get up and leave me naked in the tub, when we were supposed to be celebrating. You don't call or come to see me with a real explanation for five days, and you have the nerve to ask me how I've been and how work is? Are you for real? How the hell do you think I've been, Bryce? Do you really want to know? Or can't you tell by my red, puffy eyes? Do you really want me to tell you how work has been? You want to know all about my inability to stay focused because I've been wondering how a man who claims to love and care for me could do to me what he did for no reason at all, other than work being on his mind? Is work on your mind right now, Bryce? Do you plan on up and leaving again? Because if you do, why don't you spare my valuable time and leave now."

Monica stopped talking to take a breath and calm down. As angry as she was at Bryce, she was angrier with herself for wanting to be in his arms. "Speak goddammit!"

Bryce leaned forward on his elbows and stared down at his feet. "Baby, I'm sorry," he said softly.

"Damn right you're sorry. That was supposed to be my night!"

"I know, baby."

"No, you don't know, Bryce. I worked my ass off trying to land that account."

"Monica, I know what it meant to you."

"Bryce, if you did, you would never have left the way

111

you did! I deserved that night. I earned it. That account could very well be the turning point of my career and I couldn't even enjoy it."

Bryce's head hung lower with guilt. "Monica, I told you I'm sorry. It's just that . . ." He paused. What if this baby wasn't his? He looked at Monica, who glared back at him intensely. What if it was?

"What, Bryce? It's just that what?"

Bryce took a deep breath. "Monica, there's something I need to tell you. I don't even know how to say this."

"You open your mouth and speak."

Bryce exhaled. "I cheated on you."

Monica heard what he'd said, but couldn't believe her ears. "Excuse me?"

"I cheated on you. But I swear it's over."

Monica was speechless. He had to be joking. It had to be some type of sick game he was playing. She looked at Bryce, who did his best to avoid her gaze. She watched him clench and unclench his jaws, crack his knuckles, and rub the back of his neck. All things he did when he was nervous.

Monica could feel her eyes welling. "Bryce," she said weakly. "Is this a joke?"

Bryce didn't answer. Monica asked again, only there was nothing timid about the way she did. "Is this some kind of fucking joke?" she screamed out. "Answer me!"

Bryce shook his head no. Monica's tears began to fall. "Why are you telling me this? Why?" Tears of shame and regret formed in Bryce's eyes. They fell to the floor as he answered bluntly.

"She's pregnant. I found out last week. But I don't know if it's mine. Baby, I'm sorry."

"Get out," Monica said in a whisper.

Bryce looked up at her. "Baby, I was wrong."

"Get out!" Monica said with more force this time.

Bryce tried again. "Monica, she meant nothing to me. I love you, and I want to marry you."

At the sound of the words love and marriage, Monica shook her head. "Get the fuck out, Bryce! Get your ass out of my house!"

"Baby, please! I love you."

"Love? You don't know shit about love, you no-good dog! Get the hell out of here now. Go to your pregnant bitch. Go anywhere. Just get the fuck away from me!"

Bryce moved to try and take her in his arms. "Please Monica . . . she doesn't mean shit to me." As he got close to her, Monica hauled off and smacked him hard across his cheek. Bryce was stunned. He backed away.

"Get out!" Monica raged again. "Get your lyin' ass out. Because you don't mean shit to me either."

"Baby, you don't mean that."

"Bryce, if you don't leave right now, I swear you will regret it."

"Baby . . ."

"Stop calling me that! I'm not your baby. Your baby is waiting for you in your bitch's stomach. Leave!"

Tears cascaded down from her eyes. Her palm stung from the smack she'd delivered and she wanted to do it again. She did. She stood up and smacked his cheek again and then pounded her fists against his chest. Then she slumped to the floor into a ball, as her tears soaked her shirt and fell in droplets to the ground.

Bryce looked down at the woman he loved and opened his mouth. He wanted to say something, do anything. But what could he say that would take away her tears and her pain? He'd betrayed her trust. He'd done enough already.

Bryce took one last look at Monica as if it could possibly be the last time he would lay his eyes on her. Then he turned and left.

When the door closed behind him, Monica slammed her fist on the floor. He'd cheated. She'd loved him and he cheated and gotten someone pregnant. Monica sobbed and couldn't decide what hurt more, Bryce's unfaithfulness, or the fact that, as hard as she'd tried to avoid it, she was now in the same position as her mother.

14

Karen was glad she still had the spare key to Monica's place because the minute she walked in and saw Monica sobbing on the floor, Karen knew she wouldn't have answered her door if she'd rung the bell. Bryce had called her and told her what happened, and asked for her to go and comfort her sister. Only because she wanted to hurry to Monica's side did she not go off on Bryce. But she did take the time to call him a "pathetic lyin-ass dog." Bryce didn't respond, because he knew he deserved that and more. Before leaving, Karen told Alex what happened. Alex feigned surprise and didn't tell her that he already knew.

Karen moved to her sister. "Monica, baby," she said, kneeling beside her. Monica didn't answer. Karen wrapped her arms around her sister. Instantly, Monica buried her head in Karen's lap. "It's okay, baby," Karen whispered, gently rubbing her back. "You go ahead and let it all out.

I'm here." Fifteen minutes passed before Monica finally said a word.

"How did you know?" she asked.

"Bryce called and told me."

"The nerve of him," Monica said angrily. "I can't believe you were right."

Karen stroked her hair. "Shh. Don't say that. It doesn't matter."

Monica lifted her head slowly. "I need aspirin."

Karen stood up. "Where is it?"

"In the bathroom," Monica said, moving from the floor to the sofa.

Karen left and came back with the aspirin and a glass of water. She handed two pills to her sister, whose eyes looked like they'd gone twelve rounds with Laila Ali.

"You're wrong," Monica said after downing the medicine. "It does matter. You told me what he was doing, or in his case, had done, and I insisted that he wouldn't do that to me. I was a fool. All this time I loved and trusted him while he played me for a damn fool." Tears began to leak from her eyes again. Karen handed her a tissue. "I can't believe he did this to me. Do you know that he got some bitch pregnant?"

"He told me that too."

"Karen, all this time I thought Bryce was the perfect man, when in reality, he was nothing but a triflin' dog."

Karen sat down and placed her arm around Monica's shoulder and didn't say anything. She didn't want to add any more fuel to Monica's fire by commenting on the disgust she felt too.

"Karen, what did I do wrong?"

"You didn't do anything wrong, baby sister. Bryce is an ass, and that's all there is to it."

Tears fell from Monica's chin. She hoped the aspirin's effect would take place soon because her head felt like it was about to explode. "Just like Mama," she whispered.

"What about, Mama?" Karen asked.

"I'm just like her."

"What do you mean by that?"

"I mean I'm just like her. All this time I've put her down because she let the minister disrespect her with his womanizing, and here I am in the same predicament I swore I would never be in."

"Come on, girl. You're nothing like Mama."

"Oh aren't I? Karen, I gave my all to Bryce. I did whatever I could to make him happy, while he played me."

"But you never knew, girl."

"Maybe I did. Maybe I chose to ignore the signs. Maybe I just looked past excuses he's made in the past, no matter how weak they may have been, and convinced myself that Bryce couldn't possibly lie. Maybe I'd always seen it but tried to deny the truth."

"Maybe nothing, Monica. You are not to blame for this, and you didn't know he was fucking another woman behind your back. Don't do that to yourself. Don't put yourself in the same category as Mama. She and everyone else knew that the minister was an unfaithful bastard. She allowed herself to be the fool. You didn't. This is not the same thing."

"But what if Bryce and I were married? What would I do?"

"You would leave his ass, that's what?" Karen said.

"Would I? Could I?"

"What do you mean, would you? Girl, Bryce betrayed your trust."

"I know that, but is it really that simple? Could I just walk away from a marriage without trying to make it work? Could you walk away from Alex, to whom you vowed to stay together for better or worse?"

Karen nodded her head yes. "Monica, I may love Alex unconditionally, but after watching Mama and the minister, my answer is yes. As far as I'm concerned, infidelity is unforgivable, because once that wall of trust is knocked down, it's impossible to rebuild. And the last thing I will do is stay in a relationship where I feel I have to watch my back because I'm doubting every word he's saying to me."

Monica took a deep breath as a new wave of tears fell. She buried her head in her sister's lap again. All this time, she thought. All this time she'd judged her mother without understanding what she could have been going through. Monica fell asleep wondering if her mother had been weak or committed to her vows.

When Monica awoke, the sweet aroma of spaghetti tickled her nostrils. She slowly lifted her head from the pillow that had replaced Karen's lap and heard the clanging sound of pots and pans. She stood up easily. She still had a dull headache.

"What are you doing?" she asked her sister as she walked into the kitchen.

Standing over a pot of simmering meat sauce, Karen

raised an eyebrow and said, "What does it look like? I'm cooking us dinner."

"Karen, you don't have to do that, really."

"Too late. The food's already almost done and I'm starving. How are you holding up?"

Thoughts of Bryce's admission caused Monica's eyes to well and a lump to rise in her throat.

"I wanted it to be a bad dream, Karen," she said solemnly. She took a seat by her table. "Before I fell asleep, I prayed that when I woke up, Bryce and I would be cuddling and you wouldn't be here. But you are here, so it's not a dream at all. Bryce really did cheat on me. Another woman really is pregnant by him."

"Maybe," Karen reminded her, though it didn't make a difference.

"Yeah, maybe. But does it matter? I trusted him and he betrayed me. I feel so cheap, girl. Cheap and used."

Karen turned off the fire under the meat sauce and went to Monica, who had a fresh wave of tears streaming from her eyes. She hated to see her sister hurting like this. She put her arm around Monica's shoulder.

"I know you're feeling bad right now sis and I know it's easy for me to say this, but, things will get better and work out one way or the other. OK? Don't go feeling cheap or used.

"It hurts so bad. All I did was love him, Karen," Monica said, her torrent falling harder.

"I know, girl."

"I thought he was different, but he's not. He's just like all of the other men out there. Him . . . the minister . . .

Jeff. Why is it that the important men in my life have a knack for fooling around on women?"

Karen shrugged her shoulders and wiped Monica's tears away. "Immaturity I guess. That's the only thing I can come up with."

"I want to hate him," Monica said.

"I know you do."

"But I don't know if I can."

"I know you don't."

The sisters sat silent for a few minutes before finally eating. Later that night, Karen called Alex and explained what happened. Alex feigned surprise, again. Karen spent the night with her younger sister. In the morning, Monica woke up once again hoping to see Bryce beside her.

15

Jeff sat in his leather chair, disappointed and angry with himself. Angela McCarthy had just left his office. She was the wife of Dale McCarthy, one of North Carolina's wealthiest businessmen. Angela thought her husband should have married his job, because he spent more time there than at home. She was also irritated because they rarely had sex anymore, because her husband was usually too tired. And for Angela, a beautiful forty-five-year-old woman with the body of a thirty-year-old, not enough sex was a crime.

Jeff found it hard to believe that Dale wouldn't want to have sex with her, because he'd wanted to every time she'd come in for a session. But Angela was his patient and he knew not to cross that line. At least he used to.

His wish just came true.

Angela had been attracted to Jeff's chocolate-brown skin and his sleepy eyes the first time she'd seen him. She'd always wanted to feel his manhood deep inside of

Dwayne S. Joseph

her, giving her what her husband wouldn't. She'd fantasized about it. She'd had erotic dreams about Jeff giving her therapy from behind. She knew Jeff was attracted to her. She could tell by the way he stared at her C-cup sized breasts. That's why she wore the low-cut tops she did. That's why she wore the mini-skirts without panties. She liked to watch Jeff try and avoid taking a peek at her love box whenever she crossed her legs slowly, allowing enough time for a view.

Jeff's wish came true because Angela made it happen.

She called him pretending to be distraught and on the verge of a breakdown. She couldn't take the lack of affection. She couldn't handle being ignored. She felt unloved, unwanted.

Jeff, please help me.

Being the good doctor that he was, Angela knew that Jeff would tell her to come by the office. So she did, wearing a trench coat with nothing underneath. And when she walked into his office, locked the door behind her, and let her coat fall to the ground, Jeff's morality headed south.

After making sure his secretary had gone home, Jeff gave Angela the therapy she'd yearned for. With every prescribed thrust, Angela McCarthy moaned and smiled. She worked herself into a frenzy as she imagined her husband's reaction if he knew she'd fucked a black man. A very well-endowed Black man, who made her orgasm multiple times. A feat her husband hadn't accomplished in fifteen years. When the session was finished, Angela slipped on her coat, kissed Jeff lightly on the cheek for a job well done, and walked out of the office to go back home to her boring husband. The next time she and Dale had sex, she would imagine it was Jeff inside of her.

Jeff sat in his chair angry at how weak he'd been. He thought about Sherry and the night they'd shared together. They'd eaten the dinner he'd prepared, and before going into the living room to relax, he got down on one knee and proposed. She said yes. The rest of the night was spent in bed making love.

Jeff closed his eyes and massaged his temples. He wanted to do something he'd never done before—be faithful. He grabbed the phone and dialed a number he hadn't dialed in a long while.

"Zion Baptist Church, Reverend Stewart Blige speaking."

"Hey, Dad."

"How are you, boy? It's been a while. How have you been?"

"I've been good. Just busy."

"I know the feeling. So how's everything else going for you? You find that special woman yet? Speaking of which, are you coming to your mama's dinner?"

"I'm coming."

"Good. It'll give us a chance to catch up. You know you only live an hour away. You could come by and visit more often."

Jeff didn't respond, but instead leaned forward on his elbows. "Dad, you mind if I ask you something?"

"Of course not. You sound a little down. Is everything alright?"

Jeff hesitated for a second, contemplating whether or

not to ask the question that had been on his mind. "Dad, do you really love Mama?"

"What kind of question is that to ask me, boy? Of course I love your mama."

"If you love her, then why are you unfaithful to her?"

There was a short moment of silence before his father said, "You're out of line, Jeffrey."

"How, Dad? How am I being out of line?"

"It's not your place to ask me a question like that," Stewart said angrily.

"How the hell is it not my place? It's not like I asked some out of the way question."

"Jeffrey, I don't care how old you are, I am your father, and you will respect me as such. You hear me, boy?"

"What do you know about respect?" Jeff asked furiously. "Is that what you call what you've given Mama over the years?"

"Who are you to question me, boy?"

"I'm your son."

"That's right, Jeffrey. You're my son. My unmarried son, who has no idea what marriage is about."

"Then why don't you tell me, Dad? Why don't you help me understand how you could be consistently unfaithful to a woman who's done nothing but love, honor, and respect you?" Jeff sat back in his chair with tears spilling from his eyes.

"Jeff, why are you asking me these questions?" Stewart asked.

Jeff squeezed his eyes tightly. "I'm asking, Dad, because I have finally found a woman who means something to me. Something more than just a sex partner."

"And what does that have to do with me?"

"Everything, Dad! It has everything to do with you. I grew up watching you disrespect Mama's love. She did everything for you, Dad. She loved you and stayed by your side when other women would have left. You say you love Mama, and that she's a special woman, but you never acted like you truly meant that. You can't possibly mean what you say about her by fooling around on her."

"Jeffrey, there's a lot–"

"Let me finish, Dad," Jeff said cutting him off. "Just let me say what I have to say. Mama loves you and she cares for you. I would love to have a woman as devoted as Mama. What's sad is that I have actually found that woman, only I have one problem. Do you want to know what that is, Dad?"

"What's that Jeffrey," Stewart asked quietly.

"I can't stop being like you!"

Silence overtook the conversation as both men mulled over the last words spoken. Jeff wiped tears away from his eyes.

His father sighed into the telephone.

Jeff opened his mouth to say something that could somehow shed light to the dark mood, which now consumed them. He didn't want to be at odds with his father-too. But he could think of nothing to say that would prevent that from happening. Without a good-bye, he hung up the phone.

16

Frustrated, Bryce sat stone still, trying to think of another way to get himself focused on work. He'd already put in extra hours of overtime, by setting and accepting tight deadlines. When that didn't work, he tried taking on additional projects, which demanded more time and energy. He did all that he could with the hope that he would somehow be able to keep Monica off of his mind. But nothing worked. Monica was everywhere. In his bed in the morning, in his car sitting beside him, listening along to the loud music that he played, in hopes of not hearing her name in each verse. He saw her smile swirling in his hot cup of coffee. He saw her eyes in those of his coworkers. He couldn't escape her.

All day.

Every day.

Even in his dreams.

Bryce couldn't get the image of her crying, to leave

him alone. It beat at his conscious like a barrage of Manny Paquiao blows.

In the two weeks since he'd last seen her, he'd tried to get in touch with her. He'd left apologies on her answering machine, both at work and home. He'd called her cell phone and poured his heart out there as well, but she never returned his calls. He sent bouquets of roses, but Monica had never even accepted them to throw them away. He was miserable. He was losing weight from not being able to eat. He could barely sleep, and to make matters worse, he'd just been suspended without pay for a month. Nicole had made good on her threat and had told her father. He received no more than the month suspension only because he was one of the best programmers the company had, and possibly his boss's grandchild's father.

Bryce didn't complain.

He sat at his desk packing things he would need while away. He looked at his picture of him and Monica and wished that he could go back in time. He'd been wishing he had the power to control time a lot lately. If he had, Nicole would never have existed and Monica would have been his wife, and they'd be living happily ever after. Bryce sighed and shut down his laptop. As he stood to leave, his phone rang. He hoped it wasn't his boss, calling to tell him that he'd changed his mind, and that he didn't want Bryce to come back, regardless of the baby. Bryce picked up the phone and reluctantly put it to his ear. "Bryce speaking."

"Bryce . . . it's Monica."

Bryce's heart skipped a beat at the sound of her voice.

Damn, he'd missed her. "Monica! I've been hoping you'd call. There's so much I want to say to you."

"Save it, Bryce," Monica said coldly. Just hearing his voice rekindled the flame in her anger. She'd held up a lot better than she thought she was going to. Sure, she'd cried herself to sleep every night, but with the help of her girlfriends and Karen, she knew that what happened had nothing to do with her, and everything to do with Bryce's inability to be a real man. She didn't want to talk to him ever again, but after her mama called her to make sure she and Bryce were still coming to the birthday dinner, she knew she was going to have to call him. Her mama didn't know anything about what happened and Monica wanted to keep it that way. The last person she wanted to be judged by was her mama. Especially after all of the judging Monica had done of her. She also didn't want the minister to know because Monica was sure he'd see Bryce's unfaithfulness as some sort of victory for him. She told Karen and Alex not to say anything. She also told them that she was still going to ask Bryce to come. She would put up a façade for one weekend to avoid any talk. "I'm only calling, Bryce, to remind you of Mama's birthday dinner."

"You still want me to go?" Bryce asked stunned.

Monica exhaled. "I don't want to deal with any questions or comments from my mama or the minister. After what you've done to me, the least you could do is go."

Bryce thought for a minute. He didn't like the idea of being used, but if that would guarantee him an opportunity to spend time with her so that he could apologize and try to win her heart back, then it was worth it. "OK.

I'll go. What time do you want me to pick you up? I figure with a seven-hour trip, we need to leave at least by nine o'clock." Bryce smiled at the thought of sitting in the car with her for such a long ride.

"You don't have to pick me up. I'm going with Karen. You're riding with Alex."

"But baby, I really want to talk to you. There's so much I need to say. So much I want to explain," Bryce pleaded.

"For the last time, Bryce, I am not your goddamned baby. And I don't want to hear anything you have to say to me. Alex will call you."

Click.

Bryce breathed out slowly. He would fight, but winning Monica's heart and trust back would not be an easy battle. But he would fight for as long as he had to.

17

Alex walked into his office and saw that he had voice mail. He put down his laptop, picked up the phone, dialed his access code, and listened to the first of two messages waiting for him.

Ok, Alex. I see how it is now. Believe me, you will regret the decision you've made. I am Miguel's mother, and he belongs with me. If you think for one second that the judge is going to give you full custody, you are wrong. You having a house and making more money than me don't mean shit. I'm going to take you to the cleaners, Alex. You'll regret not sticking with our arrangement. How could you be so stupid? Oh, and until the judge makes the decision in my favor, I'm not letting you take Miguel anywhere. Get used to not seeing him, 'pendejo'!

Alex shook his head and rolled his eyes. He listened to the other message.

Why do you have to go this route, Alex? So you never met Sergio, so fucking what? As you can see, Miguel and I came

*home safely. I'm not letting you win, Alex. I don't care what de-
cision the judge might make. I'm not letting you and that bitch
win. This was probably her idea. 'Puta negra'! And Miguel is
still comparing me to her, by the way, which means that you
didn't say shit to him. That's fine. After the judge rules my way,
that won't be a problem anymore. Believe me, I'm going to win.
I just got a second job, so I'm making more money now. Once
the judge sees that, kiss your chances good-bye. You and your
wife are having a baby anyway. Now you want Miguel too? Well
forget it. You're not getting him. I am responsible, damn it. The
judge will agree. You'll see. Go to hell, Alex.*

Alex smiled. He could hear the anxiety and doubt in
Mariah's voice. She knew that Alex had a very good
chance of getting custody over Miguel. As much as she
tried to convince herself of the opposite, she knew it.
Alex was a responsible, caring father, and had genuine
love for his son. He would do anything for Miguel. And
he had. He never thought of Miguel as being a burden
the way Mariah had.

From the moment he was born, she hated the fact that
she could no longer do what she wanted, when she
wanted. She'd tried though, but Omar and Ellen weren't
having it. They forced her to assume responsibility.
Being a bad mother wasn't entirely all her fault. Because
her own mother had always been strung out, Mariah
never had a good example to learn from. She didn't
know how to show affection. She was never made number one, so how could she be expected to know what it
took to make her own child number one?

Alex had been brought up in a home filled with love
and compassion. He'd been taught the difference between

right and wrong. He hadn't grown up with the notion that wrong was right, like Mariah had. She had no father, and she had a mother who never cared that her daughter was hurting because she fell second to drugs.

Whatever.

It didn't matter anyway.

Growing up without being made a priority didn't keep Mariah from surviving, and if she could survive, Miguel could too. Alex knew that was Mariah's way of thinking. That's why he couldn't go on with the arrangement. In no way, shape, or form would he allow his son to grow up the same way as Mariah.

In a way, he felt sorry for her. She'd been a victim of neglect. She wasn't entirely to blame for the woman that she was, or wasn't. But still, once Miguel was born, Alex felt that she should have changed. Alex knew too many people who, after growing up in situations similar to or worse than Mariah's, did whatever they had to do to keep their child from going through the same pain. Why couldn't Mariah have done the same?

As Alex mulled that over, his phone rang. He looked at the ID and answered before the second ring. "Hey, beautiful. How's the mommy-to-be doing?"

"Hey, handsome," Karen said with a proud smile. "I'm doing fine. Just exhausted as usual. Work and pregnancy are an energy-sapping combination."

"Why don't you give the show a break for a while? Or at least cut back on the number of shows you do."

"No way. If Ricki Lake could do the show when she was pregnant, I can too. Besides, there is no cutting back. You know my show is live, five days a week."

"Well, just think about it. I don't want you overdoing anything. I make more than enough money to support us."

"I know, baby. But you know being a talk show host is all I've ever wanted to do. Trust me, this baby means everything to me. I won't overdo anything."

"You better not."

"Listen to you," Karen said. It made her skin tingle hearing the excitement in his voice. "Anyway, before I drop off into dreamland, I just wanted to let you know that Mariah has called here three times and left three different messages. I take it she got the subpoena to appear in court?"

"Yeah. She's left two messages here too."

"She's worried you know?"

"I know."

"Although I don't see why. It's not like she really wants the responsibility. You'd think she'd be happy you're willing to take Miguel off of her hands."

"Yeah, but she can't handle losing Miguel to me."

"You mean her pride can't handle it."

Yeah, that too," Alex agreed.

Karen sucked her teeth. "Whatever. That bitch and her pride can go to hell for all I care. She makes me so sick, with her ignorant ass. I swear I don't know how I haven't kicked her behind yet."

Alex laughed out loud. "*Calmate mujer.* You have our baby inside of you. Remember, what you feel, he or she feels too."

Karen took a deep breath. He was right. "Okay, baby. I'll stay calm. Just tell Mariah to stop calling here. I don't want to hear her damn bitching. I deleted the messages by the way."

"Not a problem. I'm sure she said the same thing on my voice mail here anyway. I'm going to save these two though. You never know if they'll come in handy in court."

"Good idea. Anyway, baby, I can barely keep my eyes open. It's time for me to go to la la land."

Alex checked his watch. It was eight-thirty. "Okay, *chula*. Hey, before you go, I've been meaning to ask you, how's Monica holding up?"

"As good as can be expected," Karen said. "She loved Bryce and his pathetic ass."

"I know she did."

"I just don't know why he did what he did. He had everything in Monica."

"Well baby, some men can keep love and sex separate. Obviously that's what Bryce did. He just waited too long to realize how much more important the love was. And remember, he's human, mistakes are to be expected."

"Well, I hope that you've already learned that lesson and that's one mistake that you won't even think of making."

"No need for me to separate, baby, because I have everything I need in you. And besides, I'm not human. I'm superhuman."

"Is that right?"

"Hey, you're the one who called me the Incredible Hulk last night."

Karen smiled as she thought about their lovemaking

from the night before. Alex had indeed been incredible and large with excitement, and if he was going to continue to work the way he had, Karen was definitely going to get all the loving in that she could.

She yawned. "Maybe on the drive to North Carolina this weekend you can pick his brain and find out why he had to go and ruin a good thing."

"I'll do that. I still can't believe she wants him to go."

"Trust me, it's better that he does. It'll avoid any drama from my mama or the minister."

"Bryce really wants Monica back. You know he's going to try to talk to her. Is she ready for that?"

"She better be."

"I hope she talks to him," Alex said sincerely. "Bryce is a good guy. Believe me, he regrets what he did."

Karen sucked her teeth. "Well he should have thought about all of that before he did his deed."

Alex decided not to go any further and changed the topic. "Anyway . . . enough of that drama. We have our own to deal with. Are you sure your mother wants me there?"

"That's what she says. Believe me, I'm still speechless."

"Maybe she's having a midlife crisis or something," Alex said being half-serious.

"Yeah right," Karen replied. "A midlife crisis is something she's definitely not having. I just hope the trip is uneventful. I don't need or want any more drama. Anyway baby, I'm about to start snoring on you, so I'm going to go before that happens."

"You go handle your business, woman."

"I love you, Alex."

"*Y yo te quiero tambien.*"

"See, it's that Spanish that got me with a bun in my oven."

Alex smiled. "I guess I better use more of it."

"You are wrong," Karen beamed. "Good night, bad boy."

"Good night, sexy."

Alex hung up the phone and felt goose bumps rise on his skin. He loved his wife with all his heart. She was his best friend, and had always been. He wished he was closer to her parents like she was to his, but with her mother's prejudiced views, that had been impossible. But maybe she was changing, or at least willing to try. He had been invited, and that was a big deal. He couldn't help but wonder why, after all this time. What was so special about this birthday?

18

A lex slammed on his brakes, put the car in park, shut off the engine, and raced out of his car. He didn't care that he'd been in a no parking zone and could be towed away. He had other more important things to worry about. The last message Mariah had left was still fresh in his mind.

Miguel is in the hospital in downtown Baltimore. I just thought you should know.

Alex was in a meeting when she'd called. The message had already been an hour old by the time he'd gotten back to his office and checked his voice mail. He raced into the hospital lobby and approached the information desk.

"My son is here. Miguel Diaz."

The receptionist behind the desk looked up at Alex and then pressed a button beside her. "Go straight back through the double doors and then make a right," she said as doors leading into the pediatrics opened up.

"Thank you."

Alex ran down the hallway, through the double doors, and then made the right. He paused when he saw Mariah near the end of the hallway, talking to a doctor. Her head was bandaged and her lip swollen. Standing beside her, was a tall, thin-framed man with a ponytail. His right eye was swollen and his left arm was bandaged. Both of their clothes were stained with blood.

Not my son, Alex thought as he walked towards them. *Please don't take my son away.* He approached Mariah and the doctor.

"Mariah, what the hell happened? Where's Miguel? Is he okay?"

Mariah didn't respond. Alex looked to the doctor. "Are you taking care of my son?"

"Yes I am. I'm Dr. Gordon. I assume you are Miguel's father?"

"Yes. Alex Diaz. Dr. Gordon, is my son okay? Where is he?"

The gray-haired doctor with wire-rimmed glasses glanced at Mariah and then looked back to Alex. "Why don't we talk a short walk, Alex?"

Alex looked at Dr. Gordon. "Look, I don't mean to be rude, but I need to see my son."

"Walk with me, Alex. We'll discuss your son's condition and I'll take you to see him. I promise."

Alex looked again at Mariah, who did her best to avoid his glare. Her friend remained silent too. He nodded to the doctor and followed him until they were out of earshot from Mariah.

"Alex, Miguel is going to be alright. He suffered a broken right arm and a couple of minor cuts and bruises. All he'll need will be a few weeks with the cast and then he'll be as good as new."

Alex let out a slow sigh of relief. "Is he awake? Can I go and see him?"

"You can see him, but I gave him something for the pain, so he'll be asleep for a few hours. But before you go, there's just something I need to discuss with you."

Alex watched the doctor with serious eyes. "What's the problem?"

"Alex, did Ms. Ortiz tell you how the accident occurred?"

"No," Alex answered bluntly. "I just got a message that he was in the hospital."

"They were involved in a head-on collision with another vehicle. Ms. Ortiz, your son, and the gentleman you saw were all passengers in the car. With the exception of your son, they all had high levels of alcohol in their system."

Alex gritted his teeth. "The driver . . . was he drunk too?"

"Yes he was."

"Where is he?"

"Unfortunately his injuries were too extensive, and we were not able to help him."

Alex nodded his head slowly. "You said it was a head-on collision. How are the passengers from the other vehicle?"

"Miraculously, the family of five suffered only a minimal amount of damage. Their car was injured more than they were."

"That's good to know," Alex said softly.

"Alex, I understand that you are upset right now, and rightfully so. But I do have to ask for the sake of Miguel and all of the other patients here, that you wait to deal with this matter."

Alex dragged his hand down over his face, nodded and thanked Dr. Gordon then turned to walk away.

But before he could, Dr. Gordon said, "I hope you don't mind me being so frank with you, but I'm divorced and have two sons. They're five and seven. I fought their mother for custody because my ex had her own idea of what responsibility was all about. We obviously disagreed. Now I know it's not in my place to judge someone, and forgive me if I'm out of line, but what I see in Ms. Ortiz is what I saw in my ex. Miguel was lucky, Alex. He's in room number five." Dr. Gordon walked away without saying another word.

Alex turned and went to see his son. Without acknowledging Mariah, he walked past her and slipped into the room where Miguel lay sleeping peacefully. He approached Miguel and lightly touched his forehead. "My son," he whispered as tears welled in the corners of his eyes. He looked at Miguel's casted arm and shook his head. He tried to ignore the "what ifs" that plagued his mind.

What if Miguel had been hurt worse?

What if he'd been the one whose life had been taken?

What if he had never been with Mariah?

Alex shook his head. He didn't want to think about that. He leaned forward and gently kissed his son's forehead and then turned around as he felt a chill come over him. Mariah was standing in the doorway, watching him silently. Guilt was spread across her face.

Alex stared at her, but didn't say a word as he opened and closed his fists. He'd planned on respecting Dr. Gordon's wishes that he avoid talking to her there, but as they exchanged glares, he found himself struggling to do so. Everything the doctor had told him about the accident and the cause, caused Alex's head to throb. He looked to his son again.

What if?

Then he moved to her, grabbed her by her arm tightly, and pulled her out into the hallway. His voice was taut and low when he spoke. "What the fuck happened, Mariah?"

Mariah didn't answer him fast enough for his liking. "Mariah, Miguel could have been fucking killed! How could you put him in a car with a drunk driver?"

"Alex . . . I'm . . . I'm sorry."

"Sorry? Please Mariah, spare me the fucking apologies. What the hell are you doing taking Miguel out with you drinking anyway?"

"We were just at a friend's house having a good time. It was late. Miguel wanted to go home. This was all his fault. If he would just have listened to me and gone to sleep on the couch like I told him, this wouldn't have happened."

"How the hell could you blame your own son for your own irresponsibility?"

"Because it's true. This was his fault. It's always been his fault. And yours! My whole life changed because of you two."

Alex opened his mouth to respond but changed his mind, because he realized that nothing he'd say would make a difference. Mariah would always resent Miguel and would never love him the way a child deserved to be loved.

As he stared down at her, he felt nothing but pity. Not only was she missing out on the miracle and joy of motherhood, but the importance of how much she could mold and shape a life never registered with her as well.

"Go home, Mariah," he finally said. "Go home and look at all of Miguel's things. Sit and look at all of the pictures you have of him. Look at the toys scattered around, go through his drawers and look at his clothes. Go home and memorize it all. Take mental pictures, because after tonight, you won't be seeing them anymore. Miguel is coming home with me."

"I'm not letting you take him, Alex!"

"Why, Mariah? To spite me?"

"Yes! I hate your ass!"

Alex folded his arms and shook his head. "You're really pathetic. It's so sad. Instead of realizing what a gift he is, you see him as a burden. And you have the nerve to try and hurt me by keeping him from me. Get out of here, Mariah. Leave and go do what I said, because Miguel is leaving this hospital with me. That's for damn sure."

"I will not let you and that bitch have him!"

No longer able to keep his cool, Alex grabbed Mariah by her shoulders and shook her. "I've had it with you and your shit. I'm not dealing with it anymore."

"Let go of me, *puto*!"

"You could have killed my son, you ignorant bitch!

You're lucky that a broken arm is all he got." He tightened his grip and closed his eyes a fraction. For the first time in a very long time he was on the verge of losing control. Not since his days in high school had that happened.

"Let go of me, Alex. Get your fucking hands off of me!"

"Yeah, let her go," a voice said from behind them.

Alex turned around to see her friend staring at him like he was about to put a hurting on Alex. Alex sized up his thin frame.

"Shut the fuck up and stay out of business that doesn't concern you!" Alex yelled.

"She is my business," the friend countered.

Alex locked eyes with him for a few seconds. Then he turned back to Mariah. He smiled at her and then without warning, let her go, spun and hit her friend with a right cross under his eye that sent him reeling to the ground.

"Sergio!" Mariah screamed rushing to his side.

"So you're Sergio," Alex said standing over them, his fists balled and itching to strike again. "Heed my warning, Sergio . . . stay the fuck away from my son. If I find out that he's anywhere near you, trust me, I will do a hell of a lot more than blacken your eye."

As Sergio's left eye bruised-up, Alex stepped past them and rubbed his knuckles. In one swing, he'd released all of the anger, frustration, and animosity he had pent up and hit Sergio the way he never could or would hit Mariah.

With his back to them he said, "Go home and do what

I said, Mariah." No more words needed, he walked back to Miguel's room, closed the door, and grabbed a chair to sit at his son's bedside.

In the hallway, no one bothered to help Mariah with Sergio. Nurses and doctors alike stood by, and had witnessed the whole event. Word of the accident and Mariah's disregard for her son's life had gotten around on the floor. Truth is, after seeing one too many children who weren't as lucky as Miguel, Alex's punch had been just what the doctor ordered.

When Mariah finally helped get Sergio to his feet, two uniformed police officers approached her. They too had seen the entire incident.

"Ms. Ortiz . . . I'm Officer Smith, this is my partner, Officer Krebs. We'd like to ask you a few questions regarding the accident."

Mariah looked at Smith, a burly black man, and Krebs, a stocky black woman with hard eyes and bowed her head. As Sergio moaned in pain, Officer Smith said, "Before we begin, we'd like both you and Mr. Tavares here to take this breathalyzer test."

Days after the incident at the hospital, Mariah had been charged with recklessly endangering the welfare of a child, and had temporarily lost custody of Miguel to Alex, while social services conducted an investigation regarding the environment Miguel was subjected to.

Alex was relieved to have his son away from Mariah, and thanked God that a broken arm was the only damage Miguel had suffered. He also thanked God for Karen, as she didn't hesitate to step in and provided love and affection that Miguel needed. Alex was worried at first about what Miguel's mood would have been since being taken away from Mariah. But to his pleasant surprise, instead of brooding, Miguel actually seemed happier. It was then that Alex realized his son had been wearing a mask for far too long. He couldn't help but feel guilty for not fighting for his son sooner.

He'd told Karen all about what went down in the hospital with Sergio and vented about how Mariah blamed Miguel for the accident. Of course, Karen wasn't surprised by Mariah's unwillingness to assume responsibility. She'd come to expect that from her. Social Services came by Alex and Karen's home to interview them and check their living conditions. Alex was more than happy to accommodate them. He had no doubt in his mind that he would now be able to get full custody for Miguel, and he had Mariah to thank for that. He would file the papers after they came back from North Carolina, a trip that would be coming up in a few days. He'd already arranged to have Miguel stay at his parents' for the weekend. Karen wanted to take him, but after the joyride he had, Alex wanted his son on house and bed rest for a few days. Yeah, he was being a little over protective, but so what. He promised he would take him on the next trip.

19

Karen guided her Lexus down the highway while Monica sat beside her staring up at the blue sky and white clouds through the tinted glass. Alex and Bryce followed behind them in Alex's Lincoln Navigator. Monica hadn't said a word to Bryce since her phone call to him. He'd tried to speak to her before they'd left for North Carolina, but Monica wasn't having it. She didn't want to hear his apologies or excuses. She would speak to him only when she had to at her parents' house and no other time, and even that she would try to avoid.

Thankfully, because her parents were old-fashioned, she wouldn't have to worry about sharing a room with him. They weren't married, so sleeping together was out of the question. Monica couldn't believe how much her life had changed in a little over two weeks.

If anyone would have told her that Bryce would turn out to be a typical man, and that she would be angry, depressed, and brokenhearted, she would never have believed it, because of the way she and Bryce fit. Together, their differences seemed to make them one complete person. After dealing with the immature, selfish, self-centered, and downright shameful attitudes of her previous relationships, Bryce had been a soothing breath of fresh air. Months after meeting him, Monica found herself drowning in the love, affection, and assurance that he provided. He was the man she wanted to marry. He was the light that she always wanted to look for to guide her when her days were dark. Now, to her dismay, that light had faded and she was painfully alone.

Monica felt her eyes watering again. She squeezed them tightly, determined not to shed any more tears. She looked at her sister, who was off in her own little world, wondering what to expect when she walked into her parents' home with Alex.

"You know," Monica said softly, "I honestly never thought I would be going back to North Carolina until one of them died. I know that sounds terrible, because they aren't terrible people."

"I understand what you mean," Karen said. "Mama and the minister really did provide for and take care of us."

Monica nodded. "I just never knew how to look past the decisions they'd made. You know I never really took the time to consider Mama's feelings regarding her marriage until Bryce cheated. I felt like I was married to him, like I'd promised 'til death do us part. But I didn't. And Mama did. And now I understand why it was never easy to just walk away from the minister, because as sad as it may seem, I'm wondering myself, if I can walk away from Bryce."

"Well, I can't tell you what to do, but I can't say that I share your revelation. You're right that they promised 'til death did they part, but in those same vows they also promised love, honor, and respect. Infidelity is wrong and a sin in the very same Bible that Daddy totes around and lives by. Infidelity is what Mama allowed.

"Girl, I recited the same vows, but believe me, I can walk away. Now, like I said, in no way am I telling you what to do. That's just me. But whatever you decide, *after* you take the necessary time, I will support you."

"Thanks Karen. I know you've been holding back your tongue—"

"Still am," Karen interjected quickly.

Monica smiled. "I appreciate it."

"Hey, you're a big girl. You have to do what makes you happy, despite what other people may feel. Just make sure you stand by whatever decision you make."

"I will. I just wish it wasn't so damn hard. He hurt me, Karen."

"I know he did, girl."

"I don't know if I can forgive and forget."

"Girl, the last thing you want to do is forget. Whether you stay with Bryce or not, you always want to remember this. Regardless of who you're with, keep it locked away in the back of your mind and use it to help keep your guard up. As far as forgiving goes, well, that depends on how strong you are and how much you love him."

"Could you forgive Alex?"

Karen thought for a minute as she switched lanes. "Girl, I love my husband. But I'm not a very strong person. I don't know what I would do. I hope I never have to find out."

Monica nodded at her sister's honesty and wondered about her own strength. She'd called her mother weak and a fool for ever staying in her marriage, but now that Bryce had betrayed her, she began to understand why her mother never left or demanded that her father leave. She loved him and vowed her life to him before God, and without having been married herself, Monica had done the very same thing with Bryce. She'd committed herself to him because she loved and cherished him, and in her eyes he was her husband. Now she found herself wondering if she could believe in that vow without having promised God that she would. Monica looked to the sky again, wishing that she could find the answer amongst the variegated clouds.

20

Sitting silently in the passenger seat, Bryce was doing his own soul searching. He had hoped to get a few minutes alone with Monica before they'd left, but it had been impossible to scale the mountain she had placed between them. With her eyes and her body language, Monica had made it very clear that his attempts would be near futile.

"Alex, you think Monica will forgive me and give me another chance?"

Alex hummed a few notes of Marc Anthony's cover of Hector Lavoe's classic, "El Cantante," and then lowered the radio. Keeping his eyes focused on the road, he said, "I don't know man. If I go by the venom she spits when she comes over, then I'd have to tell you 'Hell no!' But she's hurting, so she's supposed to call you every ugly name in the book. You just have to give it time, man. Let things die down. Let that anger inside of her fade . . . maybe then she'll be willing to give you a chance to apologize without turning a deaf ear. I wish I could give you a better answer man, but that's all I got."

Bryce clenched his jaws. "Yeah, I know it's hard to tell. Man, she wouldn't even spare a second for me to talk to her face-to-face before we left your place. I swear I could practically feel the heat coming from her. I just don't see why she can't even give me a chance to try and explain things to her. I mean, at least let me apologize."

"Well honestly Bryce, what did you expect? She's a woman scorned right now. Just be glad that all she's doing is ignoring your ass, because I know plenty of psycho women who would have keyed your car, smashed your windows, spray painted nasty messages on your front door for all the world to see, and tried to kick your balls in and cut your dick off. Believe me, there are a lot of guys who would love to trade places with you."

Although it wasn't funny, Bryce laughed. He knew a lot of guys too.

"Man, I love Monica. She's the one for me."

"Then why did you cheat on her?"

Bryce sat quiet for a moment, trying to figure out the answer. It wasn't as though Monica had been neglecting him. She wasn't selfish or frigid, she didn't drive him to drink, and she had never been overly jealous like some women. In reality, Monica was everything that he could have hoped for.

"I was a fool," he said in simple honesty. "But I realize my mistake. I want her back. Damn it, man, I need her."

"I hear you, and I believe you, but unfortunately for you, I'm not the person you need to convince."

Bryce sighed. "I hope this weekend ends better than

it's started. I don't know what it's going to be like at her parents' house, because Monica hasn't told them a thing."

"That'll be interesting."

"Yeah. I'm going to try my hardest to get her to listen to me."

"If you get the chance, you mean."

"Yeah, if she gives me the chance."

"You know that's not gonna be easy, right?"

"Yeah, I know. She's going to try and avoid being alone with me at all costs. But I have to make it happen somehow. This weekend is it."

"Do or die," Alex added.

"Sink or swim," Bryce completed.

"Well, I hope things work out for you. I'd hate to see you two officially break up. That'll be some awkward shit, because you're my boy and she's my sister-in-law. I don't even want to imagine what get-togethers would be like. Tension, man."

Bryce nodded. He didn't want to imagine it either.

"Speaking of tension," Bryce said. "I'm glad to see things may finally be working out for you with Miguel. I know dealing with Mariah hasn't been easy."

Alex smiled. "Thanks, man. It feels good having my son with me full-time. I never should have let her have him."

"Well you have him now. That's what counts. You're gonna file for custody, right?"

"As soon as I get back home. I can't wait to see my boy. I miss him already. I kind of regret not bringing him."

"Yeah, well he could use the rest anyway. You guys break the news about the baby yet?"

"Not yet. We decided to tell him when we get back."

"How do you think he'll handle the news?"

"I think he'll be alright. I think he's ready for a little sibling."

"Glad to hear. Since you mentioned being ready, are you ready to deal with Mama Blige? I still can't believe your ass was invited."

"Man, I've been thinking about that all last night and this morning. That's my Monica for the weekend. I don't know what to expect."

"Here's an ill thought: What if she invited you and had you drive seven hours just so she could tell you how much she can't stand you and Karen being together?"

"Bryce," Alex said slowly. "Don't even put that out there. Man, if she did something like that . . . let's just say that my respect-for-my-elders rule would be tossed out the window."

"I hear that. When are you and Karen going to mention the baby?"

"Sometime during the weekend."

"At least I have ringside seats for that," Bryce joked.

"Yeah. Let's just hope things go the distance. And to add to our conflicts, how do you see things going down between Monica, Karen, and their father? That's tension with a capital T. I mean it's common knowledge that he's the main reason they haven't been back to North Carolina."

"Damn! I've been focusing so much on trying to get

Monica to talk to me, that I completely forgot about that situation."

"Yeah," Alex said shaking his head. "They definitely have some real issues with their father, the great minister. Some deep resentment and anger." This is why the thought of disrespecting Karen never crossed his mind. On more than one occasion, Karen had used his shoulder for a tissue as she talked about her father's loose ways and the impact it had on her and Monica. The look of pain in her eyes had been enough to promise himself and her that she would never have to relive that embarrassment and shame. He'd assumed Bryce had done the same for Monica, and he'd been disappointed that he hadn't. But Bryce was a man, and had made a man's decision.

"Man, what have I done?" Bryce said, realizing for the first time what the effect his betrayal must have had on Monica.

Alex noticed Bryce's comprehension. "Now add Monica's feelings about her father with what you did, and that will give you an idea as to the type of weekend you may have. I have your back, but I don't envy you."

21

Jean watched through her bedroom window as her daughters stepped out of Karen's car. It had been too long since she'd last seen them. They looked the same yet different. Monica's usually vibrant face was drawn and tight-lipped as though something heavy was on her mind. There was something familiar about her look, Jean thought.

Karen had put on a couple of pounds, which was to be expected after four years of marriage. She knew her daughter wouldn't keep the weight on though, because of the show. She'd never told Karen, but she'd been able to watch her daughter's show religiously. She watched, not only because it was her daughter's, but also because it was a good show.

Jean looked from her daughters to their respective mates, who were surprisingly in separate cars. Jean took a deep breath and watched as Alex removed overnight bags from the backseat of his car. Her son-in-law, she thought. Her son-in-law who'd made her daughter happy. A son-in-law she hardly knew and had never given a fair chance. She watched him approach his wife, her daughter, and give her a hug and kiss filled with genuine love. He was a handsome man. Tall and lean, and she could tell by his smile that he was reciprocating the love that Karen felt.

She looked from Alex to Bryce. He shared the same strained expression as Monica. They'd barely spoken to one another. It didn't take a genius to figure out that they were dealing with personal issues. Hopefully they would be able to resolve their issue soon because Jean needed for everyone to be in the best of moods when she delivered her news. She turned away from the window to give them privacy.

Jeff was the only one who hadn't arrived yet. She could only hope that he would come. She needed the entire family there. For the first time, Jean realized what her stubbornness had cost her. Time. Which, she now only had a limited amount left.

Jean went downstairs to the living room where Stewart sat reading the Bible. She wondered what Karen and Monica would say when they saw him. How would they react?

"Monica and Karen are here," she said.

Stewart nodded his head. "All praises to God they arrived safely," he said solemnly.

Jean took note of her husband's position. In a way she felt sorry for him. His daughters had severed their ties with him quietly, and were now no more than strangers.

She turned away from him and checked herself in the

mirror in the hallway leading to the door. She'd done something she hadn't done in a long while—she'd put on eyeliner, lipstick, blush, and foundation. To complement the effort, she wore a floral-print summer dress and beige sandals to show off her painted toes. Change, she thought. She was overdue.

She smoothed her dress and studied herself. Prior to Dr. Johnson's discovery and diagnosis, the leukemia had been putting her body through the ringer physically, but surprisingly, she felt better than she had in a long while. Jean smiled at herself. The time had come.

22

Monica was trying her best to appear normal, but it was hard. Anger and pain had always been difficult emotions for her to mask. No matter how hard she tried to keep her mind from venturing to the gutter, her imagination would begin to work, and she'd picture Bryce naked with another woman. She'd see him caressing, kissing, sucking, and doing things she'd always thought had been reserved for her enjoyment only. Monica stood stoically beside Bryce and pushed his hand away as he attempted to take hers.

Bryce knew this weekend was going to be hard, but he was determined to get Monica to listen to him. He loved her and he hoped that she'd be able to find a way to forgive him. Although she gave him nothing but heated, contemptuous glares, he could tell that she hadn't buried her love completely. That truth only fueled Monica's frustration. *Why couldn't she just not love him?*

While Bryce and Monica struggled with their battle, Karen and Alex held hands and juggled their own thoughts and feelings. Until she'd arrived, Karen hadn't realized just how much she'd been hurt by her mother. During the course of her relationship and marriage with Alex, she'd opted to look the other way and ignore her mother's ignorance. She didn't want or need the additional stress, and she didn't want to devote any more of her time to fighting a war that she didn't want to be a part of. It wasn't until now that she'd recognized how much her mother had hurt her and just how difficult the issue was to overlook. Her own mother had missed her wedding. Not even for her daughter's sake, had she been able to put aside her intolerance.

Alex noticed his wife's hesitation to ring the bell. He looked at her and tried to give her a reassuring smile, but he too was uncomfortable. He was at the house of the very same people who wouldn't support their daughter's marriage. Their daughter, his wife, whom he loved more than they could ever imagine. He squeezed Karen's hand, letting her know that he was there for support.

Karen pressed the bell.

Jean waited before she opened the door.

Change, she thought once again.

She took a slow, deliberate breath, and then opened the door.

"My babies," she whispered upon seeing her daughters.

"Happy birthday, Mama," the sisters said simultaneously.

Jean opened her arms as her eyes welled with unexpected tears. Monica and Karen stepped into them. Neither had realized just how much they'd missed her until that very moment.

They held one another, while Bryce and Alex stood watching, silently. The three women didn't stop hugging until Stewart appeared in the hallway and cleared his throat. Karen and Monica raised their heads and stared at their father. Neither one said a word or moved. Stewart opened his arms.

"Can I get a hug from my baby girls?" he asked, forcing a smile through his hurt.

Monica didn't move as she looked at her father. The sight of him instantly brought Bryce's betrayal back to the forefront of her mind. Seeing and understanding her sister's reluctance, Karen moved away from her mother.

"Hey, Daddy," she said unemotionally. She approached her father and planted a dry kiss on his cheek. Stewart kissed her back and gave her a strong hug. He looked at Monica, who'd remained beside her mother, staring back at him with angry eyes. He forced a smile and stepped to her.

"Hi, baby," he said, wrapping his arms around her. "It's been a long time."

Monica dislodged herself from him and said evenly, "Yes it has."

Jean could feel the growing tension in the room. She looked at Alex and could feel everyone's eyes upon her, watching to see what she would do. Underneath the glow of the spotlight, she smiled and stepped to him. "Hello, son," she said, taking him in her arms.

"Hello, Mrs. Blige," Alex managed to say through his shock.

"Please call me Mama," she said, kissing him lightly on his cheek. "You are my son-in-law, after all." She tightened her embrace while Karen watched as tears began falling from her eyes. She couldn't believe what she was seeing.

Jean finally let go of Alex and looked at Bryce. "Don't think I'm leaving you out. How are you, Bryce?" She hugged him while Monica distanced herself from her father. Standing next to him had been like standing next to Bryce. She hated the fact that they had so much in common now.

Stewart noticed his daughter's maneuver but didn't say anything. He sighed and joined his wife with Bryce and Alex. "Hey, fellas," he said shaking their hands. "You guys must be exhausted."

"We're not too bad," Alex replied. "It was a pretty easy ride."

Stewart smiled. "I'd say it was an easy ride too if I came in that Navigator you have."

Alex shrugged his shoulders. "No easier than if we'd have come in that Mercedes in your driveway."

Stewart laughed heartily. "You got me there."

Alex smiled. Despite the man's ways, he could see himself having a good relationship with his father-in-law. But for the sake of going against his wife's side, and the sake of continued peace in his home, he would keep the banter to a minimum. Stewart grabbed a couple of his daughters' bags.

"Okay, fellas, let me show you where you'll all be sleeping."

"I'll come with you," Karen said, stepping beside Alex.

"What about giving Mama her presents?" Monica asked.

Jean put up her hand. "Don't worry about that right now, baby. We'll save that for dinner."

"Are you sure, Mama?" Karen asked. She and Monica had gone to the store together and purchased a white satin robe with matching white slippers, scented lotion, body spray, and soap from Bath and Body Works, a Patti LaBelle cookbook, and several other books by Iyanla Vanzant.

"I'm sure, baby," Jean said. "I'll open them later."

"Later it is," Karen said. She took her husband by the hand. "Come on, baby. Let me show you what my old room looks like." Although she wouldn't say it, she was anxious to see her old room.

"I won't see any pictures of old boyfriends laying around will I?"

Karen batted her eyes playfully. "Of course not. You know there was never anyone before you." Karen kissed him on the cheek and then bolted up the staircase. Alex chuckled and then, bags in hand, took the stairs in twos behind her.

Jean shook her head at their silliness. More than ever, she regretted having missed out on their special day. She turned to Monica. "Are you going upstairs to your old room too, chile?"

"Yeah," Bryce said quickly. "I'd like to see that old room too." He knew it was a long shot, but as long as

Monica didn't want her parents to know anything was going on, he figured she'd say yes.

He was wrong.

"I'm not ready to go up right now," she said jabbing a hole into Bryce's balloon of hope.

"You sure?" he asked.

"I'm sure," she answered, fixing a glare on him that told him she didn't appreciate his attempts. "Mama, I'll just help you in the kitchen."

Jean saw their strained interaction, and for a second she was going to try and convince Monica to go upstairs so that she and Bryce could talk. But something told her it wasn't time for that yet.

"Ok, baby. Bryce, will you tell Karen to come down and join her sister and me when she's done, please?"

"No problem, Mama Blige."

"Thank you."

"Is Jeff coming, Mama? I would have thought he would have been here already."

"I hope so, baby," Jean answered quietly.

"Is everything okay?" Monica watched her mother closely. It was obvious to her that something had gone on between Jeff and their mother. And knowing their past history, Monica could only assume they must have had an argument about Jeff and his dating preference. For as long she could remember, they'd always been at odds about that issue. While Monica wasn't too thrilled that her brother only seemed to take interest in white females, she didn't take it as harshly as her mother. Neither she nor her brother or sister had experienced anything as tragic as what their mother had to endure, so they never developed the deep feeling of resentment and distrust toward Whites. They each had white friends, both male and female, but unlike Jeff, Karen and Monica never dated anyone that was Caucasian. Alex was Karen's first time venturing into the interracial relationship realm, and it would be her last. Monica wasn't sure what realm she would be in now.

"Everything is just fine, chile." Jean walked on, without saying another word.

As Monica followed her mother to the kitchen, Bryce stared at her and wished that she would look back and acknowledge him in some way. He'd watched her closely while she'd been in her father's arms. He'd noticed her cold demeanor, and Bryce was sure that she was thinking of him and what he'd done at that moment. His shoulders slumped when she disappeared into the kitchen. She hadn't even offered an over-the-shoulder glance. He sighed, grabbed his bags, and followed behind Alex and the good minister.

23

Karen and Monica savored the aroma of the meal their mother had been preparing since the night before. It had been a long time since either one of them had eaten a real down-home cooked meal. Because of their busy lives, they'd rarely been able to really devote the necessary time to the kitchen the way they'd been taught to.

Turkey was baking in the oven, rice with black-eyed peas was simmering on the stovetop, and collard greens and corn bread were already prepared and were cooling.

Jean smiled as she watched her daughters inhale the fragrance through their nostrils. It felt good to have them there. Home felt like home again. "Girls," she said, sitting down by the island in the middle of the kitchen. "Get away from that stove and come sit with me."

The sisters reluctantly moved away from the stove and joined their mother.

"We should have been the ones preparing this meal

for you, Mama. This is your day," Karen said, sitting to her mother's right.

"She's right, Mama," Monica agreed. "You're supposed to be taking it easy and relaxing."

Jean nodded her head. "I am taking it easy, girls. And Lord knows I don't cook like this for just your daddy and me. This is relaxing for me."

"But it's your birthday, Mama," Karen said.

"So? Does that mean because it's my birthday I can't cook?"

Karen shook her head. "No, but–"

" 'But' nothin'. It's my day, and I wanted to do this. Days like this don't come too often. So now that we have that settled, how have you girls been? It's been too long. There's so much to catch up on. Karen, how is your show going?"

Karen smiled proudly. "The show is doing really well. I think I'll be taking it national soon. I've been talking to people from the TBS network."

Jean beamed and looked seriously at Karen. "Karen, I never told you, but I am addicted to your show. I've been watchin' the show every afternoon. You gon' be like Oprah soon."

"Mama, how do you get to see that out here?"

"Chile, some months back, Mr. Parsons from next door installed a satellite for us for free."

"Isn't that illegal, Mama?" Karen asked.

Jean looked at her daughter and winked. "Chile, if it wasn't meant to be, the good Lord wouldn't have made it possible for me."

Karen laughed. "You know that's not right, Mama."

Jean shrugged her shoulders and played innocent.

"Well I'm glad you like the show, Mama."

"Chile, I'm proud of you."

Jean turned her attention to Monica. "What's wrong, baby?"

Monica shook her head slowly in an attempt to say nothing was wrong, but Jean wasn't having it. "Chile, I am your mama. I gave birth to you, cleaned your dirty behind, and raised you." Jean took Monica's face in her hands. "There ain't nothin' you can hide or keep from me. Now I saw you in distress the minute you all arrived, so you may as well talk."

Monica shook her head half-heartedly and tried, but couldn't keep tears from snaking down her cheeks. "Mama, why did you stay married to Daddy?"

Jean looked at Monica. So did Karen. "Where is that comin' from, chile? Why are you cryin'?"

"Mama, you don't have to pretend that Daddy was a saint, because we know he wasn't. We know all about how he disrespected you by being with other women. I know you must be hurting over it, because Bryce did it to me too, and I feel like I'm dying inside. Why did you stay with him, Mama?"

Karen handed Monica a napkin and took her sister's hand.

Jean sighed and spoke to both of her daughters. "Girls, I love your daddy. And I promised God I would always love him through the good and bad times."

"But he ran around on you so many times. Mama, that's not what those vows are about," Monica said.

"None of us are perfect, chile."

"Damn it, Mama," Monica snapped. "It's not about being perfect. It's about giving and receiving respect. When you promise to love someone, you promise to respect them too. Daddy never gave you that, yet you stayed with him. Why? Mama, betrayal hurts so much. Why did you live with it?"

"Chile, I made a promise to God, and on top of that, I had a family to take care of."

"But Daddy—"

"'Daddy', nothin'! Baby, no matter what a woman does, or how good she is, sometimes men will just be men. All a woman can do is hope that a man gets to a point where they realize that they have to grow up. That's their decision to make, and that's something that can't be forced. Eventually most men get to where they're tired of bein' little boys. Baby, I'm sorry Bryce did what he did. But he's a man. Now, you as the woman have to decide if you love and believe in him enough to move on. Do you love him, baby?"

Monica closed her eyes; she wanted to hate him. "Yes," she said softly.

"Okay then." Jean got up from the table and went to the stove. Stirring the pot of rice, she said, "Love is a wonderful thing, girls. And when it's real, it can hurt like hell sometimes." Jean closed the lid on the rice and without a word, walked out of the kitchen, leaving Monica and Karen to ponder the things she'd said.

Jean wanted to be alone for a few minutes, but before she could make it to the stairs to go up to her bedroom, the doorbell rang. Her heart stuttered as the chime faded away.

She walked to the door slowly. *Praise God, he'd come.*

She opened the door and looked from her son to his companion. Tense silence hovered around them for a moment, before Jean looked at her son and smiled. "Hello, Jeffrey."

"Hello Mama," Jeff answered quietly. He'd thought about not coming to the dinner. He thought it would have been better had he not been there. But something happened to Jeff that hadn't happened in a long time.

The Lord had spoken to him.

It had been through one of his patients, who'd just lost his mother. Grieving over the loss, Ken Murphy said, "I never got to tell my mother how much I loved her. Or how much her presence meant and helped me. I know you're supposed to be the one helping me with my depression and giving me advice doc, but take it from me, don't make the same mistake I made."

Jeff understood the message loud and clear, and on that day, decided that he had to make the trip.

"Mama . . ." he said, turning toward Sherry. "This is Sherry. Sherry, my mama."

Jeff watched and waited to see what his mother would do. He decided to bring Sherry, despite his mother's feelings. Sherry was important to him and his mother would have to see that.

Jean's heart beat slow and heavy. She looked at Sherry and forced herself not to see an image of four white teenage boys beating on a girl–one she'd conjured in her mind over the years–but rather the beautiful woman standing before her. She extended her hand. "Hello, Sherry."

Sherry took her hand. "Hello, Mrs. Blige. It's nice to meet you. Jeff has told me so much about you."

Jean smiled pleasantly and looked towards her son, who stared back at her with disbelief at her cordiality. "Well, he hasn't told me anything about you, so you'll have to tell me all about yourself."

Jean held Jeff's gaze for a few seconds, then she fixed her attention back on Sherry, who was delightfully attractive. "I'm sure my son has told you all about me. Unfortunately, it's very true. But it's time to change."

Sherry smiled. "I appreciate your honesty, Mrs. Blige."

Jean stepped to the side. "Come inside, please." When she closed the door, she said, "Jeff, your daddy is in the living room with Bryce and Alex. Dinner will be ready in about thirty minutes. You men set the table. Everything you need is in the dining room."

Jeff nodded but didn't move. His mother's cordiality was something he hadn't expected. It worried him. "Are you okay, Mama?"

"Chile, it's my birthday. Now go say hi to your daddy and you men get that table set. Sherry, come let me introduce you to my daughters."

Jeff watched his mother lead Sherry to the kitchen and then turned to see his father step out of the living room. Both men looked at one another but didn't say a word, as their last conversation replayed in their minds.

"Jeffrey," Stewart finally said.

"Dad."

"Glad you could make it."

"Glad I came."

Silence again as the two men contemplated what to say or do next. Jeff thought about his patient's advice again. He opened his mouth to say something, but before he could, Stewart said, "Come into the living room. Alex and Bryce are there."

Stewart turned and walked away without waiting for his son. Jeff sighed and followed behind. Maybe they would try again later.

24

"Monica, can I speak to you for a minute, in private?" Bryce asked, stepping into the kitchen. Monica gave Bryce a hard, unfriendly glare and didn't respond. She hadn't meant to say anything to her mother about what Bryce had done, but the pain had been too hard to hide. Now that she had, she wished that she'd never asked Bryce to come. "Please?" Bryce pleaded. He could feel the vehemence coming from her, but it didn't matter.

Jean put her hand on Monica's shoulder. "Go out back, chile."

Monica exhaled, then stood up and walked out through the back door without saying a word.

When Bryce stepped outside and closed the door, Monica, who had walked to the old swing set her parents had bought for their children years ago, said with her back to him, "I don't want you here, Bryce."

Bryce's shoulders slumped. "Baby, please, can you at least hear me out?"

"I don't want to hear anything you have to say. You've said enough already."

"Monica, I'm so sorry for what I did. Baby, you've got to believe me."

"Do I know her, Bryce?" Not that it would make her feel any better, but she couldn't help but wonder if the other woman had had any opportunities to smile in her face.

"No," Bryce lied. Nicole had actually met Monica at a company picnic. Bryce knew better than to tell the truth.

Monica curled her lips. She didn't know whether to believe him or not. She turned and faced Bryce. She had another burning question to ask, but she wanted to see his face when he answered. "When was the last time you saw her?"

Bryce lowered his chin to his chest and inhaled. This wasn't the conversation he'd wanted. "Monica . . . does it really matter? It happened and now it's over. I want to talk about us."

"Us?" Monica snapped. "And what do you mean 'does it matter'?"

"I don't want to talk about the past. I want to focus on the future," Bryce said hoping her voice wouldn't raise another octave.

It did.

Monica's neck stiffened. "I don't give a fuck if it's the past! You fucked some other bitch, and you got her pregnant! I have a right to know all about your shit. Where did you fuck, Bryce? On her bed? On yours? Or did you use the spare key and fuck on mine? How many times, Bryce? How many times did you two fuck while you were telling me that you loved me? Did this bitch even know you were involved? Or did you play it up and tell her you were single, in which case, she would just be another one of your victims? How did you do it, Bryce? Tell me goddammit! When did you find the time to fuck and make babies? Was I around? Or did you do it when I went away on business? Is that it? Your pathetic ass waited for me to leave town to get your swerve on, while I sat up in a hotel room missing you and thinking how lucky I was to have you? Tell me, you lyin' ass coward!"

Monica paused to wipe away tears, which ran in rivulets down her cheeks. Her head was pounding from the pain Bryce had caused. Her hands shook with anger.

Bryce looked at her and felt his heart shattering. He couldn't deal with knowing he'd hurt her this way. "Baby, please . . . I'm sorry. I love you."

Monica shook her head furiously. "How did she get pregnant, Bryce? Did the condom break? Or did you love me so much that you fucked her without one? Is that how much you loved me? Speaking of which, are there any other baby mamas I need to be worried about?" Monica wrapped herself in her arms. "My God," she whispered. "I have to go and get a blood test. You could have given me AIDS!–"

"Monica," Bryce cut in. "I don't have AIDS."

"How the fuck do you know?" she said viciously. "Have you been tested? Has your bitch? Damn it, Bryce, I loved you! Do you hear me? I gave you my heart and the only thing you could do with it was break it. I hate you now, Bryce. I fucking hate you! I want you to leave. I don't want you at my parents' home. I should never have asked you to come."

"Baby," Bryce pleaded. Tears were falling from his eyes now. "Please give me another chance? I don't want to lose you. I love you. I need you."

He took a step toward her. He desperately wanted to wrap her in his arms and hold her for eternity.

Monica stepped back and put up her hands, letting him know that eternity no longer existed. "Don't come any closer, Bryce. And don't use the word love anymore. At least not with me. Save it for your ho."

"Baby–" Bryce tried again.

"Leave Bryce. It's bad enough my father is here. The last thing I want is you here too. Leave! Get your shit and go!"

"Monica, how am I supposed to get home? We're in North Carolina." Bryce asked weakly.

"I don't give a damn! Take a bus or walk home. As a matter of fact, call your damn baby mama. Just leave." Monica turned her back to him and wept powerfully. Bryce wiped his tears with the back of his hand and took another step toward her.

"Monica . . . I love you so much. You're my world. My everything. I made a mistake. Baby, please, we can get through this. I know it. Just give me a chance."

"Get the hell away from me!" Monica hissed.

Bryce shook his head defiantly. He didn't want to give in. "I need you," he said in a barely audible whisper. A couple of more steps and he would be able to hold her. If he could just do that, he could make everything right again, but before he could move to her, a voice called out from behind.

"Bryce, please respect my daughter's wishes."

Bryce closed his eyes and lowered his head. "But I love her," he said defeated.

"If you love her, respect her," Jean said, walking past him to her daughter's side.

A new wave of tears fell from Bryce's eyes. He'd lost. He took one last look at the woman who was everything to him, the woman whose body was shuddering from her sobs. He looked to Jean with pleading eyes. Give her time, Jean mouthed without a sound. Bryce nodded and exhaled. He'd done his crime and his sentence had been delivered in callused rejection.

Give her time.

Did that mean there was a still a chance?

Bryce walked back into the house to get his things.

In the yard, Jean held her daughter firmly and allowed her to cry. She'd heard the whole conversation from the window after ushering Karen and Sherry out of the kitchen. Monica was her daughter, so of course she would listen. She'd heard too, the comment Monica had made about her father. Jean hugged her child and kissed her forehead. She never wanted any of her children to feel this type of pain. Pain that she'd been all too familiar with, and had grown numb to. She squeezed Monica tighter. It was now time to speak to the family.

25

"I have leukemia. Doctor Johnson has given me up to two years to live, but that's with medication and chemotherapy. But I'm not takin' any medicine and pollutin' my body with radiation is not an option, so the most I'll probably survive will be six months to a year, give or take a few months. The timeline is for the Lord to decide."

Jean sat down while everyone at the table stared at her in stunned silence. Ticking from the clock hanging in the kitchen was the only sound that could be heard.

Stewart watched his wife, searching for some type of indication that she had been joking. "Jean; baby . . . are you serious?" he asked, his jaw slack, his eyes wide.

Jean looked at her husband. "Yes," she answered evenly.

"Wh . . . when did you find out?"

"Last month."

"Last month?" Karen asked.

Next it was Monica to speak. "You mean you knew that long and didn't tell us?"

"I'm tellin' y'all now."

"Like this?" Jeff asked.

Jean placed her hands on her hips. "How else should I tell you?"

"I don't know, Mama," Jeff answered. "Just not like this. We came to celebrate your birthday."

"And what do you think I'm doing? I am celebrating."

"Celebrating what, Jean?" Stewart asked angrily. "You find out you're dying and you don't even bother to tell me in private? I'm your husband damn it!" Stewart rose from his chair and threw his napkin into his empty plate. "How could you keep this from me?"

"Sit down, Stewart," Jean said unflustered by his anger. Stewart and everybody else stared intently at her, each lost in their own thoughts. "Sit Stewart," she said in a more forceful tone.

Stewart sat down reluctantly. Monica shook her head. She'd had enough pain to last her a lifetime. "Why are you doing this, Mama?"

"Chile, I'm not doing anything but passing on the news the Lord done already delivered to me."

"Why like this, Mama?" Karen asked in a pain-filled voice.

Jean took a sip of her juice. "Everyone, I'm sorry you all had to find out like this, but I couldn't tell you any other way."

"You're not making any sense, Jean," Stewart said, his fists clenched. "How could this be the only way to tell us?"

"Life for me changed after Dr. Johnson gave me the news, and I don't mean changed because I'm dyin'."

"Don't say that, Mama," Monica said loudly. "There are treatments, medicines . . . something. They can clone animals for Christ's sake. You're not dying!"

Jean touched her daughter's hand. Her eyes were fixed on her husband as she said, "I'm dyin'. This leukemia is not curable. I'm dyin'. But it's okay."

"How can you say it's okay, Mama?" Jeff asked, fighting tears. Sherry sat uncomfortably beside him.

"It's okay Jeffrey, because I've finally done something I needed to do a long time ago. Change. That's why I wanted you all here. There are things I need to say to each and every one of you. You too, Sherry."

"But Jean–" Stewart started.

"Be quiet and let me finish Stewart. You can at least do that for me."

Thrown by her acerbic tone, Stewart became silent. Jean stood up again. She'd dreamt of this moment since finding out about her infliction. Only in her dream, her heart had been racing and her palms sweaty. Now that the moment had finally arrived, she was surprisingly calm.

"Monica, I know that you don't agree with the decisions I've made regarding your daddy, but I made those decisions for me. Yes, he's disrespected me, and yes, I allowed it." Jean paused to make sure she had her husband's attention. The numb stare on his face let her know that she did.

She continued.

"But like I said, I had a family to take care of. Sometimes

179

as women, we have to make tough decisions, as you now know. Chile, those decisions are even harder when you have a family to raise and when you truly love someone.

"Baby, you don't have a family, but you, yourself, said that you love Bryce. I know you're hurting right now. But it will get better. I promise. The pain will lessen. But give Bryce a chance, baby. Maybe not today, or even next week, but give him one. Because I can see in his eyes that he does love you. He's a man, baby, and he made a man's mistake. You got to give him at least one chance to make up for it. Believe me, chile, that's not being weak."

Monica nodded her head slowly as her mother's words sank in. For the first time she'd realized how strong of a woman her mother truly was. "I love you, Mama," she said softly.

"I love you too, baby."

Jean turned her attention to Karen and Alex. "Karen, you know I came up in a different time. I've seen and experienced some difficult things. Things that I could not get past. Because of that, I robbed myself from enjoying the most important day of your life. Baby, I love you and I ask for your forgiveness for not coming to your wedding. Alex, I'm sorry for not being able to look past my own ignorance and realize that my daughter would not settle for anything other than the best to be at her side. You love my daughter in a way a man should love a woman, and when I look in her eyes, I can see that she is truly happy and she loves you. Alex, I love you for brightening my baby's world, and so I ask for your forgiveness too."

Alex smiled. "Thank you, Mrs. Blige. It took a lot to do what you just did. And you never needed forgiveness from me."

"Thank you, baby. And please, call me Mama, or Mama Blige. You're family." Jean looked at Karen, who sat silent with tears of joy and sadness running down her cheeks. "Baby? Will you forgive me?" Karen stood up and walked to her mother. "I love you, Mama," she said wrapping her arms around her.

"Mama, there's something Alex and I need to tell you," Karen said glancing at her husband. He nodded. "We're having a baby."

Jean clasped her hands together and looked up to the sky. "Thank you, Jesus," she whispered. She kissed her daughter again and then called for Alex to come over. He did, and she hugged him tightly. It's about time one of my children gave me a grandbaby."

"But Mama, that means that you can't leave," Karen said.

Jean smiled and kissed her forehead. "My departure time is in the Lord's hands, baby. Now go sit down. I'm not finished yet." When Karen and Alex sat down, Jean looked at her son. "Jeffrey, it's no secret that I've had a problem with you and your dating preferences. Sherry, my mama was murdered by four white teenage boys because of the color of her skin. They didn't care that she was a beautiful and kind woman, who was loved by all. It didn't matter that if my mama had come across either one of them while they were cold and starving, she would have readily given up her coat or taken them in for shelter. See, my daddy told me that's the kind of woman she was. But those boys didn't care. She was a nigger and they hated her.

"Jeffrey, as wrong as it was, I've carried the exact same type of hate deep in my heart for years. Even though the Lord said it was wrong to hate, I let it consume me, and because of that, I've wronged you. Now I've been given a chance to make amends, because instead of taking me from this earth without hesitation, the Lord gave me leukemia. I couldn't leave this life behind without telling you that you are my son and I love you unconditionally. You are and have always been a good boy. Who you choose to date is not for me to judge, but for me to support. Baby, you have that now. Sherry, if my son cares for you enough to bring you here, then I care for you too."

Sherry smiled and said a soft, "Thank you," while Jeff stood and went to his mother. He never thought this day would come. "Mama, you can't leave," he said, taking her in his arms. "Sherry's going to marry me. You have to be there."

Jean hugged her son tightly and then made motion for Sherry to join them. Sherry rose from her chair and did.

"You take care of my son, you understand me?" Jean said, holding on to her.

With tears flowing from her eyes, Sherry said, "I will. I promise."

Jean hugged her son and Sherry while everyone smiled.

Everyone except Stewart.

He sat silently in his chair, staring at his wife who was dying. His wife that he'd never been faithful to, yet who continued to love him. He'd recited the very same vows before God and their family, yet it wasn't until now that he'd finally come to grips with how much of a hypocrite he'd been.

Jean watched him staring back at her while Jeff and Sherry went back to their seats. Silence took center stage within the dining room and the spotlight was now shining on the head of the household. Karen held Alex and Monica's hands. Jeff held onto Sherry's.

"Stewart," Jean began in a soft yet unyielding tone. "I love you. I have since I first met you. Because I loved you, I married you and vowed to be your wife until my death. Stewart, as I always have, I'm going to keep to those vows, but because you've never been able to do the same for me, I've decided to move on."

Stewart's mouth opened slightly. "Move on? What does that mean?"

"I can't stay with you anymore, Stewart. If Karen and Alex will have me, I'll be moving in with them where I can be close to my grandchild." Jean looked at Karen who was too stunned to do anything but nod.

Stewart rose from his chair. "Jean, you are my wife, and you will not be moving anywhere!" he said sternly.

"Yes, I am your wife, Stewart! I have stayed by your side and played the doting wife, who looked like a fool in everyone's eyes, while you romanced every, and any woman that would have you."

"Now hold on a minute—" Stewart cut in sharply.

Jean slammed her hand on the tabletop, causing juice to spill from a few of the glasses. Stewart as well as everyone else watched her with surprise. Never had she been so animated with him. "No, you hold on a minute, damn it! All these years went by and I allowed you to disrespect this entire family. It's one thing to make me the laughing stock of the congregation and our friends, but you did it to our children too."

"Our children?"

"Yes, our children. Why do you think Karen and Monica left North Carolina to go to school hours away from here and never came back?"

Jean paused and looked at her daughters, who couldn't believe she'd known. "You two never had to say why you left. I'm your mama, and I've been around the block. I know more than you think I know. Stewart, you provided for your family and made sure we never went without, but what you did was what you're supposed to do when you have a family. If you truly wanted to be a man Stewart, then you would have practiced what you preach every Sunday. You are a good man, but you have a lot of growing up to do. And I simply don't have the time to grow with you anymore. I did what I had to do with this family, and now it's time for me to live my last few months on this earth in happiness."

Jean looked around the table, nodded her head, and then left the hushed dining room and went outside. She stood in the middle of the yard and took a long deep breath of fresh evening air. She held the air in her lungs, savoring it for a few seconds, then released it slowly, along with the weight she'd been carrying upon her shoulders.

She was dying, but she'd never felt more alive than at that moment. She dropped to her knees and cried.

With all eyes on him, Stewart stood contemplating what had occurred. He looked from his son to his daughters and cleared his throat. In their eyes he saw the painful but very real truth, which he had tried to deny for so long. He'd been the cause of the separation of his family. He cleared his throat again, then walked out of the dining room and went back to his favorite chair in the living room. He sat down and exhaled.

His wife was leaving him.

Stewart closed his eyes as tears leaked from them, and silently began to repent for his sins.

26

Bryce sat in the greyhound station waiting for his bus to take him back to Maryland. The cab he'd called after leaving Monica's parents' house had dropped him off an hour ago. He still had another two hours to wait.

He clenched and unclenched his jaws as a picture of Monica crying on the ground appeared in his mind. He could see her tears, feel her pain. He ground his teeth together and exhaled slowly. The weekend wasn't supposed to go that way. While he knew they weren't going to be where they were before, he'd at least hoped to have been on the road to resolution, no matter how bumpy it may have been. As long as he and Monica stayed on track, he would suffer through the dips and potholes. He would deal with the cracks. But he never got the chance, and now he was alone, contemplating a life without the woman that he loved.

He looked to his right at a couple who sat with their

hands intertwined. They talked quietly and smiled at each other. Bryce could see the love they shared in their eyes. He sighed and looked away. Their happiness only reminded him of what he'd lost.

His thoughts went next to Nicole and the baby. He still had no idea if it was his. The prospect of fatherhood set free different emotions. On one level he felt anxiety. He never wanted to have a child to a woman that he didn't love. He didn't want to go through what Alex was going through with Mariah. He didn't want to be bonded to Nicole in the way Alex and Mariah were bonded to each other.

But even as he dealt with anxiety, he couldn't deny that he was feeling pangs of excitement as well. He could quite possibly be the father of a child. A child that would follow his example, a child who would depend on him for the rest of his/ her life. As unfortunate as the situation was, there was joy to look forward to knowing that his existence could be more important than ever. But with the joy and stress, there was still the regretful knowledge that Monica may not be a part of his life to stand beside him. *Wait*, Mama Blige had said. How could he?

He grabbed his cell phone and dialed Monica's number, knowing that she wouldn't answer. He hung up when her voice mail came on. He thought again about Mama Blige's words to him. She said that if he loved Monica, he would respect her wishes and leave. Bryce did love her, and so he left. But he regretted his decision. He closed his eyes and breathed slowly.

Wait and respect her wishes. Fight for her love.
Which was the right thing to do?

As he battled with his decision, an announcement came over the PA system:

Attention Greyhound passengers, please listen to the following announcement carefully. The 6:00 bus to Baltimore, MD has broken down. All passengers waiting for that bus must now take the 4:00 bus to New York City, which will now make the stop in Baltimore. The bus is located in gate B, and it is now boarding and will be departing in fifteen minutes.

Bryce sat quiet for a long while. He wanted to rip his ticket to shreds. He looked toward gate B. No one had moved in that direction. Bryce stood up and grabbed his bags and walked to the bus.

27

Karen stood outside in her parents' backyard and caressed her belly, which now had a slight bulge. In a few months she would feel her child kicking, turning, and attempting to prepare for birth. She smiled at the thought of experiencing that. But as quickly as the smile came, it disappeared just as fast.

Her mother was dying.

Karen looked up to the sky through teary eyes.

"Hey sis," Monica said, coming behind her.

Karen turned to see her sister walking toward her. "Hey."

"It's warm out tonight."

"Yeah. It is."

"Remember when we used to come out here and look up to the sky, searching for our favorite singers?"

Karen smiled at the recollection of their attempt to find their *stars*. "How could I forget?"

"We were stupid," Monica said with a laugh.

"No more than every other kid at that time."

"True. Remember when Mama would have to force us away from here to go to bed?"

"Yeah, I remember. What was it you used to say to her?"

Monica laughed. "I would whine and say, "But, Mama, if we go to bed now, we gon' miss our stars. And Michael Jackson is the biggest star there is."

"And Mama would always say, Chile, if you don't moonwalk your behind into this house, I'll show you stars alright.' "

Both sisters laughed heartily now, thinking of the innocence of their youth.

"Mama always did put us in our place back then," Monica said.

"What do you mean us? I was the oldest. I got it the worst."

"Hey, I wasn't as spoiled as Jeff was."

"Yeah, well I still got it worse."

"Listen to you," Monica said playfully tapping her sister's arm.

"It's true though, and you know it."

"Whatever."

Both sisters got quiet then, looking upward and listening to the concert of the night created by the crickets and the subtle breeze blowing through the trees.

"It doesn't seem fair, does it?" Monica asked, breaking the silence. "We go all these years at odds with her and just as we resolve our issues, we find out she's being taken away from us. Why did it have to happen this way?"

Karen placed her arm around her sister's shoulder.

Monica continued on. "You know there was a lot about her that I didn't understand. I never realized what she put herself through, what she endured for our happiness. I was unfair in judging her."

"We both were," Karen said softly. "We both didn't understand a lot of things."

"I saw nothing but weakness in her. I never gave her the credit she deserved. She hung in there for all of us, all our lives."

"You know, I wanted to hate her for not coming to my wedding. I wasn't able to be completely happy that day because she didn't come."

"I know. I remember the look in your eyes. I saw behind your smile. Do you think she would have accepted Alex if she weren't . . . dying?"

Karen didn't respond right away. She caressed her stomach and thought about her sister's question. She wanted to say that yes, her mother would have eventually come to her senses because she wanted to do what was right for the family. Karen wanted to smile and say that without a doubt the leukemia had nothing to do with her mother's sudden approval of her marriage, but she knew that she could not.

Her mother wouldn't have changed were it not for the diagnosis. That very honest, but painful admission should have lessened the joy she felt now that her mother had finally welcomed Alex into her heart, but it didn't. Thanks to the leukemia, Karen had finally been able to get what she'd wanted years ago—her mother's complete support.

"No," she said finally answering Monica. "But it doesn't matter."

Monica nodded and placed her palm flat on her sister's belly.

"Mama's dying," she said with finality.

Karen placed her hand on top of her sister's. "Mama's dying," she repeated.

Jeff stood by the kitchen window and watched his sisters. He wanted to join them, but he decided against it. His mother was dying; his sister was having a baby. With every passing is a birth. He sighed and watched his siblings. Now that his relationship with his mother was on a road to recovery, he wanted to work on getting closer to Monica and Karen. They'd never been as close as they could or should have been, although that was his fault. His mother's news made him realize how short and unpredictable life could be. God had given him the opportunity to bond with his family again. He would just have to put forth the effort. He followed his sisters and looked up toward the sky. Somewhere within the black sea, his mother's new home was being prepared.

28

Stewart stood at his podium just as he had for so many years and said not a word. The choir had just moved the souls of the dead and the living with the harmonic blend of their voices. The congregation stomped, clapped, felt the spirit move through them and now they were ready for their minister's testimony.

Stewart stood before them, silent and worn. He hadn't slept a wink all night. He still couldn't believe that Jean was dying. He couldn't help but feel as though the leukemia had been brought on by his inability to be the husband that he should have been. That, if he'd never given in to the beckoning of flesh, death would never have been a topic at the dinner table, and she would never have made the decision to leave.

Stewart repented his sins in his chair in the living room, in the darkness and vowed to never stray again. The next morning, despite his prayers, after Jeff drove off, Jean said good-bye and left with her daughters to head back to Maryland, leaving him alone.

Stewart looked into the faces of his parishioners. He looked at the women, a few of whom he'd bedded. They stared back at him, each with their own private memory of their moment in time. Stewart looked into their eyes, hating himself for his transgressions. For the hurt and disrespect he'd caused his wife and children. For the shame he'd brought to his family. He cleared his throat and leaned forward into the microphone. He'd thrown away the sermon he had prepared on the joy of love. Joy of anything was the last thing he wanted to discuss. He looked into the congregation once again, hoping by some small miracle to see his wife and children there. But as he expected, they were not present.

"Brothers and sisters," he started slowly. His heart was aching, his mind struggling to bring forth the words. "Do you ever just say you're sorry? Do you ever apologize for the wrong you've done?" He paused for a second, watching as many of the church members nodded their heads that they had. "Apologizing isn't always easy to do. It's not always easy admitting when we've done wrong to each other. We have to swallow our pride sometimes to do it, because let's face it, no one likes to be wrong. But we all do wrong things. The funny thing is, when we sin, we assume that we're hurting only other individuals, but that is not true. Because when we sin, we hurt not only other people, but ourselves as well. Did you realize that?

"A sin is an infliction to the soul. And it doesn't matter how big or small the sin is, because they all have the same effect. Little white lies, the lies we tell the most, are just as damaging as one big lie because those little white lies add up. How many of those do we all tell, brothers and sisters? How many times do we inflict ourselves or others? I wish it were the case, but none of us are perfect. We all sin, so again I ask you, do you ever just say sorry? Sorry for the lies, the sin, the pain?

"Trust me, good people, someone right now is hurting because of something you've done or said, or didn't say or didn't do. You may be that person. Sorry. It's only one word, but it can be so powerful. And just like everything else, that word can be abused. So when you say it, you must make sure you mean it. Sorry. Say it with me, brothers and sisters. I'm sorry."

"I'm sorry," the congregation repeated.

"Say it louder. I'm sorry!"

"I'm sorry!" everyone belted out again.

"Louder! For those who aren't here, for those who can't hear you, I'm sorry!"

"I'm sorry!"

"For those you've lost, for those who deserved to hear it years, weeks, days ago. I'm sorry!"

"I'm sorry!"

"I'm sorry!" Stewart yelled out again as his knees buckled and he dropped to the ground.

"I'm sorry!" the worshipers said again.

On his knees now, tears spilling from his eyes, Stewart screamed, "I'm sorry!"

The congregation repeated the words again, but softer this time.

"I'm sorry! I'm sorry!" Stewart yelled yet again, his shoulders slumped. His body shook. His tears fell. "I'm sorry!"

No one spoke this time, but rather watched in stunned silence as their minister sobbed before them.

Stewart didn't care that he had an audience. His wife was gone, his children were gone. His sins were to blame. "I'm sorry!" he yelled out again, his voice weakening. He said it one more time, desperately hoping that Jean would hear. He whispered it again and again until someone came beside him and touched his shoulder. He looked up, praying it would be his wife.

It wasn't.

Stewart bowed his head as he was helped to his feet and led away from the altar.

29

Six Months Later

Karen tiptoed into the room, careful not to wake Alexia Jean, her precious gift born a week before her mother passed away. Karen smiled as she watched her bundle of joy sleep heavily just like her daddy did.

Alexia Jean was born at 12:00 A.M. on Christmas Day. Karen's mother passed away in her sleep at 12:00 A.M. on New Year's Day. Karen lightly touched Alexia's forehead.

Giving birth had been a seven-hour ordeal of back splitting, Alex-this-is-your-damn-fault, intense pain. Pain that she hoped would be easier with the next child, because she and Alex planned on having at least two more. Karen marveled at the rhythmic rise and fall of her daughter's tiny chest. It was her turn to be a mama now. She remembered the feeling that overtook her the moment she held Alexia in her arms. She'd never experienced anything as incredible or powerful as the devotion and love she felt for her child. There in the delivery room with Alex beaming proudly beside her and their six-pound baby girl in her arms, she understood the passion with which she'd heard women say they would die for their children. As Alexia cried in her arms, she knew she would do the same.

Karen sighed.

She missed her mother and wished that she had tried to prolong her time amongst them. Since the dinner, Karen, Jeff, and Monica all tried to convince their mother to do just that. But despite their pleas, Jean refused. She wanted to use whatever strength she had left to help Karen through the pregnancy. Chemotherapy and other treatments would have robbed her of that chance by leaving her weak and bedridden.

Even with that, the siblings remained persistent and without their mother's knowledge, paid a visit to Dr. Johnson's office to see if there was something their mother could have taken that would slow the leukemia down and leave her with strength.

Karen and Monica had to make the trip back to North Carolina, but they didn't mind. There in the doctor's office, the three siblings had the same question.

"Dr. Johnson, is there anything that can be done to keep our mother alive?"

The doctor regretfully shook his head. "I wish I could say that there was, but unfortunately your mother's leukemia is too far advanced."

The siblings didn't respond for a few seconds. They'd

all hoped for a different answer, though they knew the possibility would be slim. Jeff cleared his throat and slid forward in his seat.

"Doctor, we've all done a lot of research on our mother's CLL, and we know that if we can't do anything to get rid of it, there are at least special treatments or medicinal combinations that can be tried to slow its progression down."

The doctor nodded his head. "You're correct, there are. And I've tried to get your mother to listen to the different options. But she made it perfectly clear to me that she didn't want to explore any of them, and honestly, I think she made the right decision."

Karen spoke this time. "Doctor, as you can see, I'm pregnant. My baby will be our mama's first grandchild, and we'd all like for her to be present when he or she is born. I don't see how her not trying something . . . anything to live longer is the wrong decision."

Dr. Johnson leaned forward on his elbows and formed a steeple with his fingers. "I lost my mother to lung cancer a couple of years ago. My mother smoked two, almost three packs a day religiously for as long as I can remember. Hell, I wouldn't be surprised if she smoked a couple while giving birth to me." He paused and smiled at his joke. "Anyway, when she found out about the cancer, just like your mother, it was in its very advanced stages. It had actually spread beyond her lungs to other areas of her body.

"Like you all, I wanted my mother to live. I wanted her to see my children grow up and have children of their own that she could possibly get to know. And just like I told you all, I was told by her doctor, that the cancer was so advanced that any treatments she would undergo would have a very slim chance of being effective. But despite the doctor's advice, I still convinced my mother to try radiation therapy. And just like the doctor said, it didn't work."

"But at least she tried," Karen interjected.

The doctor nodded. "Yes she did, but you know what? There is not one day that I don't regret my persistence."

"Why?" Monica asked.

"My mother suffered to get better. The radiation that was supposed to help, crippled her body and spirit far worse than the cancer ever did or could."

He paused, reflecting on the memory of his mother's pain.

"I watched my mother lose her hair. I was helpless as days went by where she couldn't move, couldn't eat, could barely speak. Sleeping was her only comfort and even that had been laborious for her. Now I know that you all want to do whatever is in your power to keep Mama Blige alive for as long as possible. And believe me, I would like for that to happen too. But I have to be honest. I think she made the right decision in declining the treatments. She is dying. She is going to die. I know that seems harsh to say it so bluntly, but it's the only way to say it because it's the truth. And believe me when I tell you that for Mama Blige's sake, you have to accept that. Because if you don't, you will continue to do just what you are doing now—lose time trying to prolong a life that will end. Believe it or not, there is a positive to this ordeal."

"And what would that be doctor?" Jeff asked.

"Mama Blige is not dead yet. Go and enjoy the time that you have with her now."

After leaving the doctor's office, though it was hard, Karen did just as the doctor had suggested and enjoyed her time with her mother. She took a hiatus from the show and enjoyed days with her mother, enjoying all of the sights Baltimore and Washington, DC had to offer. Jean helped Karen endure what had been a difficult pregnancy, and along with Alex, with whom she had become very fond of, made sure her daughter's needs were taken care. Although she herself had been in great pain and at times extremely weak, she refused to allow Karen to go overboard with anything.

At times Karen actually became frustrated over all of the fawning. "I'm pregnant, not handicapped!" she would say.

Jean would simply ignore her cries and continue doing her thing. She wanted to see her grandchild before she passed, and if that meant that she would have to continue to treat Karen as though she were crippled, then so be it.

For all of the whining Karen did, she truly didn't mind her mother's fawning. When Alexia was born, both Jean and Alex were in the delivery room.

Karen had grown accustomed to her mother's presence, as they'd grown closer than they had ever been. With a newfound respect for the things her mother had said and done, she'd seen a side of her mother she never knew existed, and she was proud.

She'd only spoken to her father once after the dinner.

He'd called to check on her to make sure she was okay. The telephone conversation lasted only fifteen minutes. Weeks after Jean's birthday dinner, a twenty-five-year-old member of the church claimed Stewart to be the father of her three-month-old baby boy. As much as he wanted to, Stewart couldn't deny the child's spitting image.

Ashamed and embarrassed, he stepped down as minister of the congregation and distanced himself further from his family. He wasn't present when Alexia was born, and Karen didn't see him until her mother's funeral, which consisted of only the immediate family, because that's how Jean wanted it. Stewart came to pay his respects and say his final good-bye to his wife who kept her vow, but severed all other ties.

Jean wanted her last months to be her happiest, and they had been. She'd reconciled with her children and she'd seen the new addition to the family tree. What more could she have asked for?

Karen blew Alexia a kiss and smiled. She'd signed a contract with TBS and her talk show was now televised nationally. Add to that her adorable baby girl, a husband to whom she knew she would grow old with, and a mother who would always watch over her; it was easy for her to say that she was blessed.

Standing in the doorway, Alex stood silently watching her. With the reconciliation with her mother, Karen was finally truly happy, and that made Alex feel good, because in his mind, his wife deserved nothing less. He too missed having his mother-in-law around. She'd become his true second mother, nagging and complaining whenever she felt the need. And like any good grandmother, she also made it her job to help keep Miguel in line. Alex never had to go to court for full custody over Miguel. A couple of months before Alexia's birth, Mariah and Sergio were involved in another head-on collision. Again, they had both been drinking, but unlike the last time, they both died.

Alex cleared his throat softly to announce his presence. Karen turned around and smiled at her man.

"Hey beautiful," Alex said, quietly walking into the room.

"Hey yourself, handsome," Karen whispered, welcoming the kiss he planted on her lips. "How was work?"

Alex passed his hand through his hair. "Too long and filled with too many idiots. But it's nice being back on my normal schedule though."

"Yes it is," Karen agreed. "I was getting tired of not having my man next to me at night."

They hugged and then Alex leaned over the bassinet to see his daughter. "And how is my Alexia?"

"Sleeping—finally," Karen answered. "And please let's keep it that way. That little girl is definitely your daughter. Geez, can she whine."

Alex laughed softly. "I'll show you whining," he said patting her behind. "Where's Miguel?"

"He's spending the night at his friend's from school."

"Good. I was a little worried about how Mariah's death was going to affect him."

"Yeah, I was too. It was rough on him at first, but he's a tough kid. It's a slow process, but he really seems to be adjusting to life without her."

"Well you and Mama Blige had a lot to do with that."

"More my mama," Karen said softly. "You know . . . I really miss her. I never thought I would ever say that. It's amazing, but that one dinner seemed to erase everything that had been wrong and made it all right. My mama did that," Karen said proudly.

"She was a strong and special woman," Alex said.

"Yes she was. I only hope I can be half as strong for Alexia, as she was for us."

"Well you won't have the same type of issues to deal with, but believe me, you are already plenty strong."

"I love you, Alex," Karen said throwing her arms around his neck.

"And I love you, Karen."

They kissed gently for a few seconds before they were interrupted by Alexia's crying. They looked at one another and laughed. Karen patted Alex's behind. "I've had her all day. Go do your thing, *papi.*"

30

Monica stared at the phone in her hand and wondered if she would be able to make the call. Lord knows she wanted to over the past six months, but she wasn't ready. At least not as ready as she knew she needed to be. Her mother told her to wait and give her heart time to heal. Then, if it had healed enough, she could make the call.

"But how will I know when it's healed enough, Mama?" she'd asked.

"When you can no longer stand bein' without him."

Monica took her mother's advice seriously. After the events unfolded, Monica had come to understand, admit, and appreciate that there was much about life that she still had to learn, and that there was no one better than her mother to learn from.

Monica had come to respect her mother like never before. She watched her mother fight and eventually lose her battle with the leukemia. She came to admire her strength, as her mother lived her life until the very end, never allowing the disease to get the best of her. Monica cried an endless stream of tears the day her mother died. In a very short span of time, her mother had become her teacher and her friend. And thanks to the Lord's mysterious ways of working, because of Bryce's mistake, mother and daughter shared a special bond of understanding and solidarity.

When the casket was lowered into the ground, Monica knew then that she was ready to call Bryce. Jean had known all along that she would, because she knew what real love was and how strong its power could be. And she knew it existed between Monica and Bryce.

Monica wiped a teardrop from her eye as an image of her mother appeared in her mind. She sighed and hit the talk button on the phone. Her mother had said to give Bryce a chance.

She dialed his number.

Bryce, who'd been miserable and lonely since leaving Monica in tears, checked the caller ID before answering the phone. When he saw who was calling, his heart beat heavily. He'd been praying for this call. He took a deep breath, held it for a few seconds, and then let it out slowly and answered the phone on the second ring. "Hello?" he said calming the excitement in his voice.

Monica took a deep breath. "Hello, Bryce."

Bryce smiled at the sound of her voice. "Hello ba . . . Monica," he said quietly. "How have you been?"

"I've been good. How have you been?" *God, his voice,* she thought. *Had it ever sounded sexier?*

"I'm good . . . now. I've missed you."

Monica smiled but resisted the urge to tell him how much she'd been missing him too, and how she longed for him, his touch, and his company. "Did I catch you at a bad time?"

"Not at all. I heard about Mama Blige. I'm very sorry. I wanted to come to the funeral, but I heard it was just for the family." His voice trailed off. He never thought he would have been on the outside of that circle. Monica wiped another tear away. Alex had told her he'd spoken to Bryce. Despite the breakup with Monica, he and Alex had remained close friends. At the funeral, Monica had prayed that Bryce would show up.

"At least she went peacefully," she said.

"Yeah. I heard she got to see Alexia before she passed."

Monica nodded her head and beamed. "Yeah. The Lord definitely granted her last couple of wishes."

There was a long pause then as they both struggled with what to say next. Bryce wanted to apologize again for what he'd done, how he'd hurt her, but because he didn't want to bring any negativity into the conversation, he remained silent.

Monica had a question that she wanted to ask, but she just didn't want to know the answer. But she had to know. And she wanted Bryce to tell her, which is why she never brought up the topic with Alex. She hesitated, knowing that whatever happened from this point, hinged on the answer that he would give. For a split second she regretted calling.

"How does it feel to be a father?" she finally asked. Her heart beat thunderously as she waited for Bryce's response.

Bryce opened his eyes wide. "A father? Didn't Alex tell you?"

"Tell me what?"

Bryce squeezed his eyes tightly, bit down on his lip and smiled. "I'm not a father. The baby wasn't mine." He left it at that and didn't mention that Nicole had been fooling around with another coworker. She'd hoped that the baby would be Bryce's, but she was never sure. Bryce's boss apologized and gave him a raise for the stress his daughter had cost him. It was also given with the understanding that Bryce would not pursue anything legally.

Goose bumps rose from Monica's skin. He wasn't a father. She pulled the phone away from her ear, covered her face with her hands, and cried tears of relief. Bryce heard her through the receiver. He knew then that he hadn't lost her.

Monica cried for several seconds more and then came back on the line.

"Bryce?" she said, her lips quivering, her voice a soft whisper.

"Yes, baby?"

"Come over."

Bryce looked up to the ceiling and mouthed a thank you. "Fill the bathtub," he said. He hung up the phone and got up to get dressed. Now that his prayers had been answered, he would make his second chance count.

31

Jeff stood with his hands clasped behind his back and stared out of the window, which was being reprimanded heavily by rainfall. The dreary weather reflected the mood he'd been in since finding out Sherry had been playing him. He'd been nothing more than a tool designed to make her ex-boyfriend jealous. He wanted to be angry with her for her deceit, but he couldn't. When he showed up at Sherry's house back from his business conference a week early, and caught her straddled over her ex in her swimming pool, moaning with pleasure, he did nothing but ponder the irony of his life. What he'd spread around had finally come back around. Jeff laughed and without disturbing the two, walked away from Sherry. God had finally given him his just desserts.

But his lack of anger didn't stop him from being hurt. He'd let his guard down and he had paid for it as he always feared he would. But in spite of it all, he knew that he would not rebuild the wall. Love was out there for him somewhere. And it would come in its due time. Perhaps from the attractive sister he'd met at the conference.

Jeff had his mother to thank for his new outlook on life and love. In the time she had left before her death, she made sure that her bond with her children was the strongest it could be. She was especially determined to get to know her son, with whom she'd had the most strained relationship.

Jeff was glad for the time he and his mother had. Before her passing, he'd come to truly understand how much of a gift life was. And he realized that love was a delicate and priceless miracle. And thanks to his sisters and his mother, he came to understand and appreciate the strength, determination, and beauty of a black woman.

Jeff turned away from the gloom outside and faced his father, who lay in the hospital bed, weak and dying. After the sermon he'd given the day after the birthday dinner, Stewart began to drink himself to sleep every night in his empty house. As strong as his faith was, he was still a normal man. The emotional abuse he'd caused his family had finally come to a head, and he lost his wife not once, but twice. To make matters worse, a church member came to him with a son that he couldn't deny even if he'd wanted to. One night, the weight from the stress and pain had become too much for him to bear, and he had a stroke. Had Jeff not come by to visit that evening, he would have died.

Jeff stared down at his father. He thought about his days as a child and how much he'd respected and looked up to him. Part of the man Jeff had become, he'd owed to his father. And while he had qualities he wasn't always proud of, Jeff could not deny that his father had done a hell of a job.

They'd never settled things after the argument they had, and as much as he wished they could, Jeff knew they would never get the opportunity, because he knew that the doctor's efforts to save him would be in vain. Jeff knew that his father was a broken man, and no longer wanted to go on. Jeff touched his father's hand.

Stewart, weak from the trauma, struggled to look at his son. He wanted to tell him that he loved him, and that he was sorry for the pain he'd caused, but all he could do was stare. Father and son held each other's gaze and spoke without words, expressing the love they shared. Then Jeff leaned forward, kissed his father on the forehead, and walked out of the hospital room. He would call his sisters soon to tell them their father had moved on. They would bury him next to their mother, where husband and wife would finally be of one flesh.

End

Book club discussion questions

1. Do you think Jean's decision to remain in the marriage all of those years had been the right decision? Was she truly strong?

2. Do you think Stewart truly understood what type
   of an effect his womanizing had on his family?

3. How did you feel about the relationship between
   Jean and her children? Who was more at fault for
   the strain with them—Stewart or Jean?

4. How did you feel about Jean not trying to extend
   her life by taking medication or seeking special
   treatment?

5. In your opinion, what was the main theme of the
   novel?

6. If put in Monica's position, would you have taken
   Bryce back?

7. Do you think Stewart would have gotten closer to
   his children had he lived?

8. Has Jeff really changed his ways, or will Sherry's betrayal cause him to revert?

9. How would you feel if your child wanted to marry someone of another race?

10. Would Jean have ever fixed her relationship with Karen, Monica and Jeff without the diagnosis of the leukemia?